Mack is [illegible]
make n[illegible]

Bolan's body was sh[illegible] ack fabric, and he walked as silent as th[illegible] The Executioner had become a part of the night.

"Hey there," he said softly as he moved across the elegant expanse of lawn.

"That you, Sid?" said the hardman, cupping a match in his hands to light a cigarette. "You're a little late, but I guess there's some left for you. I was first in line for her."

"Good for you," Bolan said, and shot the man in the head.

In the front room two more men were staring mindlessly at TV, with plates and sandwiches in their laps. One was raising his sandwich to take a bite when Bolan said, "Over here," in the flat toneless voice of death. The man turned and stared; his mouth was still gaping when he swallowed a tumbling bite of eternity. His pal dived toward a sofa, where a submachine gun lay propped against the cushions; Bolan helped the guy along with a whizzer through the neck.

Bolan went up the stairs. He pushed open a door and saw the fat man, sitting at a desk. "I think you've made some mistake..." whined the man.

Bolan leveled the AutoMag and fired.

About the author

Don Pendleton is a much decorated veteran of World War II who saw action in the North Atlantic U-boat wars, the invasion of North Africa, as well as the assaults on Iwo Jima and Okinawa. He was also among the very first Americans to land in Japan just before the surrender, and he later served in Korea. He has since worked in the missile and aerospace industries.

An author of wide experience, he has captivated millions of readers with the compelling drive and absolute credibility of his writing. In ten years, Don Pendleton's Executioner books have become bestsellers in many languages throughout the world. In Mack Bolan, Pendleton has created a classic modern hero big enough to take on the most powerful forces of crime and terrorism.

"Mack is not a mindless killer," says the author. "He is proclaiming that humanity is important, that it does matter what happens here, that universal goals are being shaped on this cosmic cinder called earth. Bolan is an American hero whose actions are fast and effective. I only wish the world had more men like him, leaders with commitment, principles, dedication and bravery—the so-called old-fashioned virtues that were so evident in 1776."

MACK BOLAN

THE EXECUTIONER 40

Double Crossfire

DON PENDLETON

A GOLD EAGLE BOOK FROM
WORLDWIDE
TORONTO • LOS ANGELES • NEW YORK • LONDON • PARIS • SYDNEY

Published January 1982

ISBN 0-373-61040-8

Special thanks and acknowledgment from the author to Steven Krauzer for his contribution to this work.

Printed in U.S.A.

There is no week nor day nor hour when terror may not enter upon this country, if the people lose their supreme confidence in themselves, and lose their roughness and spirit of defiance. The only bar against it is a large, resolute breed of men.

—Walt Whitman

Plant your stealthy bombs that maim little children, then call it a glorious war of liberation if you can. But I call it simple savagery, and I will stop you. I can respect any true soldier under whatever flag, but you murderous terrorists fill me with disgust. I have more respect for a cockroach, and I will step around it. But I will not step around you....

I will grind you into the earth.

—Mack Bolan

To the more than one million Armenian people slaughtered in the holocaust of 1915-1918, and the many millions of others of all nationalities who have become victims of homicidal hatred in our time, this book is dedicated.

PROLOGUE

Mack Bolan was a veteran, a soldier of long service. He fought in a war he didn't choose, in Vietnam. And he fought in a war he did choose—in fact, he designed it—against the Mafia. This last seemed to be an endless war, from mob to mob, city to city. But after thirty-eight bloody campaigns, the Mafia Wars did come to an end, of sorts. In New York City. To underworld survivors it was also the end of their scourge, the man known as Mack Bolan, the Executioner.

But not really. Only the name was put to rest. And a new identity born, John Phoenix. It would be the same man, with a newer and larger war.

Destiny shaped this return. There would be more battles to be won and campaigns to be concluded, but there'd always be a war. Tactics and terrain might differ, but the enemy and the war would always be there. Always that evil force, that devil's antithesis to humanity's growth and progress... from the plunderers and highwaymen of yesterday, to the international terrorists of today.

For every few steps mankind takes forward, there is a faltering step backward. For every positive action, a negative reaction. For every injustice, a final justice. It seems to be the eternal yin and yang of life itself, which is, after all, the ultimate justice.

Mack Bolan was a messenger of justice, a keeper of the balance. A man who preserved life by dealing with death. A man who continually walked the unmarked line of truth and morality. Morality? Yes, man is a moral agent. Mack Bolan knew that to be true.

The human mind seemed to be structured toward a moral awareness, an intrinsic recognition that some things are right and some are not—and structured, also, toward the need and the desire to establish and maintain standards of conduct.

It was perhaps the most worrisome aspect of human understanding, while also the noblest. Out of that need for ethical standards had been born all the world's religions, all its politics, philosophies, traditions, customs—all the things that bring us together while also dividing us as contentious factions.

And, yes, the human mind was designed for contention, too. That was our guarantee for individuality; the guarantee, also, of conflict forever as individual minds debated the definitions of good and evil.

If Mack Bolan had been inclined to think of such things, the stoic warrior could probably recite an endless succession of critical moments when moral dilemmas could have destroyed or neutralized him. Because Bolan was indeed a moral agent. Not the type who would stand at podium or pulpit to verbalize his moral perceptions but the sort who would silently incorporate them into a life-style. The kind of man who could not pay lip service to an ethic while otherwise ignoring it.

He made his individual judgment on the Vietnam dilemma and staked his life there while passing no judgment whatever on those who found a different moral answer. He did it again, back in the jungles of home, more alone than ever and more committed to a harsher ethic, when his Mafia Wars brought him into direct opposition with the collective precepts of the American nation—and, again, he did it without feeling the need to debate the matter with those who disagreed.

He could do so because Mack Bolan was a man at peace with himself; his wars were external, not internal, conflicts, his principles a pattern for living, not mental exercises. And he was at peace with himself because somewhere along his road of life he had found a higher understanding than most of us encounter in our day-to-day lives. It is written in Bolan's journal:

> Not only is man a moral agent, he is the only moral agent in the entire perceptible universe. The struggle, then, is a cosmic struggle. . . with cosmic goals. It is both Alpha and Omega. John Phoenix, you'd damn sure better never forget it.

John Phoenix was, of course, Bolan himself—the cover name under which all past "sins" against the nation were expiated. And the admonition to the self is very telling to the character and motivations of this remarkable man: he was saying, in effect, that moral dilemma is the shaping force of human evolution, the primary cause and the ultimate effect of human life. He was saying that the human mind is structured by nature for war everlasting.

The New War had begun. The battles would be many. The enemy would be everywhere. The weapons would be as primitive as the fist, as modern as the laser. Last time it was the jungles of Colombia; this time it was the barren wastelands of Turkey; next time it might be the streets of a major city, or the very place assumed to be impossible.

Yeah, morality had nothing to do with it. Only everything.

1

Mack Bolan came up behind the guy soundlessly, and if he hadn't deliberately let one hand knock against the side of the van, the guy would never have seen the face of his executioner. As it was, he was clearly startled, and he tried to cover it with talk. That was a mistake. The guy wasn't used to talking and acting at the same time. It was a mistake all right—the last one the guy ever made.

"Nice rig. Thought I'd take a look..." he said vaguely, and then he tried to move on and bring up the gun in his right hand at the same time.

But Bolan's own right hand was already emerging from under his left arm to level the Beretta Brigadier on the man from nearly point-blank range. A silenced 9mm Parabellum slug drew a pencil-line of light through the night air, and the guy's face changed. Below, his mouth opened wide in a look of surprise and dismay.

Above, a raggedly torn third eye leaked red from the middle of his forehead.

Bolan got the door of the van open, dragged the guy up the steps, and dumped him in the back. He had been out of the rig less than forty-five seconds, going EVA via the rear door while the guy was nosing around the front.

Nobody had taken any notice of them. It was dark, and besides, in Beverly Hills nobody was ever about on foot night or day.

Bolan reseated himself at the control console and checked the monitors. There was no sign of additional activity at his primary target, the house across the street. It was large, even by the standards of this wealthy suburb just west of Los Angeles proper. The red brick of its Georgian architecture made it look even larger, somehow more massive. Nearly an acre of immaculately tended lawn swept down to the sidewalk, beyond which towering palms lined the parkway next to the street, Benedict Canyon Drive. A long black-topped driveway arced up one side, passed under a portico shading the front door, and came back down on the other side to the street.

Bolan parked the van in front of a slightly smaller and more modern-looking house. There was apparently a party going on, because several other vehicles, mostly sports cars, were parked at the curb. The van fit right in. On either side of it, a vaguely psychedelic scene had been air brushed in full color. It also featured oversized bubble windows with tinted one-way glass, wide tires with raised white lettering, a sliding sun roof, and a lot of superfluous chrome. It was just the thing that a Beverly Hills partygoer with $30,000 or so to spare might be driving.

The dead hardman lay in a crumpled heap against the back door where Bolan had dumped him. He was a big man, several inches over six feet and at least 200 pounds. He had a dark complexion and wore a bushy mustache and dark hair cut short. Bolan went quickly through his pockets. He found a loaded spare clip for a .45 automatic in the coat, a dirty pocket comb in the pants, and nothing else. The polyester suit the guy was wearing had come from a popular discount chain store. The back of it was slick with gore from the exit wound that had taken off most of the rear one-third of the gunner's skull.

In a way Bolan was grateful to the guy, whoever he was. He had just confirmed what Bolan had suspected all along.

This one had turned into a hard-probe, and someone was determined to see that Bolan didn't live to see it through.

There would be others. Bolan had no doubt of that, but he felt instinctively that for now the numbers were on his side. There had been no back-up man working behind the guy whose brains were now messing up the van's floor. If there had been, Bolan would have heard from him by now. They'd figure him dead then, and they'd take their time with whatever was about to come down. When it did, Bolan would be waiting for them.

A good-looking man came out of the front door of the party house, carrying a drink and weaving slightly. Bolan recognized him through one of the tinted port-windows; he had seen him on the cover of one of those celebrity-interview magazines. The guy was the star of some kind of detective series. The man looked around, as if he were waiting for someone to come up and breathlessly demand his autograph. When no one did, he took his drink and himself around the side of the house. From its back came the sound of a woman's squealing laughter and then the splash of someone diving into a pool, or maybe falling in. The party sounded in full swing.

But Bolan wasn't interested in the party, except as a convenient stroke of camouflage. It was that Georgian mansion across the street that had brought him to California on this balmy early spring evening.

There were cars parked there as well, but they were accommodated by the long driveway. In contrast to the sports cars among which Bolan had taken his place, these were Cadillacs and Mercedeses, with one Volvo and a Jaguar sedan thrown in—ten cars in all. As Bolan watched, a latecomer, a long-nosed Rolls-Royce, pulled up to the head of the line. A middle-aged man in a business suit got out of the back compartment and entered the front door of the house without ringing. A chauffeur in livery backed the car into the line, then got out and lit a cigarette.

Bolan lit one of his own and turned his attention to the compact but complete electronic console at which he was seated, a little state-of-the-art wizardry courtesy of Herman "Gadgets" Schwarz. In fact, the van itself was part of the L.A.-based Able Team's surveillance fleet, on loan to Bolan during what he expected to be a brief visit to the City of Angels.

Bolan flipped a toggle switch, his hands moving quickly and surely. The bundle on Bolan's floor had buddies, and they'd be on scene sooner rather than later. In whatever time he had left, Mack Bolan wanted to acquire as much advance intelligence about the situation as he could. In thirty-eight campaigns against the grasping tentacles of the Mafia octopus, and now again in his new war against the burgeoning threat of international terrorism, Mack Bolan had learned that careful planning and surveillance, not mindless wild-ass heroics, was the key to victory over these jackals.

Above Bolan's head, the van's sun roof slid open, and a small directional antenna rose into the gathering dusk. Bolan twisted a miniphone into his right ear, then worked the large knob that controlled the antenna rotor. Static started to clear as the signal strength meter centered itself, and then a man's voice came through clearly.

Bolan clicked on the cathode ray display tube at his left elbow. The screen brightened, then resolved into a computer-generated floor plan of the first story of the house. Both the plan and the "bug" were courtesy of Able Team member Rosario "Politician" Blancanales, who had planted several of the tiny transmitters and reconned the house that afternoon, posing as a Pacific Gas and Electric repairman tracking down a short circuit somewhere in the neighborhood.

The man's voice was deep and rich, with no trace of an accent. "My friends," he was saying, "you have perhaps guessed why I asked you here this evening. I have spoken with most of you before; all of you have surely heard of the World Armenian Congress. I hope to be able to explain to you tonight the Union's work and answer any questions you might have about it, in hopes that you will be moved to support the group with both your personal endorsements and your financial generosity."

On the CRT a blot of light was blinking in one room of the floor plan. The room was set toward the back of the house and to Bolan's left, as he faced it. Pol had described it as some sort of conference chamber, dominated by a large oak table seating about fifteen men.

The speaker's name, Bolan knew, was Marko Adamian. He was the owner of a large import-export business specializing in petroleum products, heavy machinery, and electronics—a sort of superbrokerage that had made Adamian a millionaire many times over. Unfortunately, Adamian was not confining his international activities to business matters. Although the man was American-born, both of his parents had been driven by Turks from their native land in what was now eastern Turkey and had emigrated to the United States via Syria around 1920. As a result, Adamian, like many Armenians, both fervently supported Armenian nationalism and had a virulent hatred of Turkey. Unlike most of his countrymen, however, Adamian was getting involved with some pretty unsavory company in pursuit of his ideals. And right now it looked as if it was up to Mack Bolan to keep the industrialist's butt out of the sling.

"I think," Adamian went on in Bolan's ear, "that all of us may reasonably call ourselves influential men, both in the Armenian community and in our adopted country as well. All of you surely know Mr. Djirdjirian, and of the successes of his film company. Senator Sarkesian's efforts in the state legislature have resulted in advances and recognition of our people all over California."

The introductions were half over when a red signal light next to the CRT started to flash. Bolan flicked a selector switch. Simultaneously, the transmission from the bug inside Adamian's house was input directly to the tape recorder, and Bolan's earphone and the console's microphone were cut into a special radio circuit.

Bolan quick-scanned the setup and said, "Go."

The nasal voice of Gadgets Schwarz sounded in the earphone. "I've got Hal standing by on landline, Sarge, ready to patch him in if you can take it. Hal says it's Priority Red."

"Hal" was Harold Brognola, top federal cop and Bolan's liaison with the Oval Office of the White House. "Put him through," Bolan said.

"You got him, Sarge."

The deep, level voice of Hal Brognola came on cool and calm, but Bolan knew this man well enough to hear the edge of excitement cutting through. "We've got confirmation from our regular intelligence channels, Striker," Brognola said, using the code name which he had bestowed on Bolan during the Mafia campaigns. "Adamian's in up to his neck, all right, and I don't like any of it."

"I had a little confirmation myself, Hal," Bolan put in. He quickly explained about the attempted breach of the van's defenses, and the deadly result—deadly for one terrorist hardguy, that is.

"That means it could be going down any time," Brognola said when Bolan had finished.

"Any minute," Bolan corrected.

"Right," Brognola said crisply. "That's why I'm glad I made contact. I'll try to make it short and to the point."

"It might have to be."

"Here's what we've got," Brognola said. "There is a direct link between Marko Adamian and an operation in Turkey that we've been monitoring for some time. And the Turkish operation is tied to the KGB."

"And that means a direct link to the Kremlin."

"Correct. A smuggling pipeline is being set up, and the same names keep cropping up on that angle as on Adamian. We are pretty certain that Adamian is being suckered—I'll have more details when I see you back here—and that makes it worse. The guy may be idealistic and overcertain of himself, and too blind to see when he's playing with fire, but he's also an American citizen, and we've got to make sure someone doesn't get it into his head to blow the guy away."

"Well, it looks like he's been targeted," Bolan said.

"That fits in with the rest of it," Brognola said. "Again, details will have to wait. But we do know now what the smuggling pipeline will be carrying."

Bolan waited.

"Heroin, Striker," Brognola said. "Enough to flood the streets of every major American city."

Bolan sensed more than heard the car pull up across the street from him. Moving to his left put him in front of one of the oversized windows, which was opaque from the outside but afforded an excellent wide-angle view from where Bolan sat.

"It's going down, Hal," Bolan cut in.

"Number and ID?" Hal said immediately.

"One carload so far," Bolan said. "No ID I'm off the air, Hal."

"Live large, buddy," the head fed got in before Bolan broke the radio link.

No ID, yeah. But a tentative make, for sure. The car was a black Cadillac limousine, the kind that could carry eight using the twin jumpseats in the rear compartment. It was cruising very slowly along the curb under the palms in front of Adamian's mansion, the motor chugging softly, the car long and sleek and sterile in what was now the full darkness of evening.

It looked familiar.

It looked like a Mafia warwagon.

And then a door must have been cracked open, because the dome light came on. Bolan could hear the angry snarl of a man's voice, and immediately the door slammed shut and doused the light.

But not before Bolan got a look at the man at the end of the back seat. There was something strange about the side of the face Bolan saw in profile. It was scarred, or somehow disfigured, but not so much that Bolan could not recognize it.

And yeah, he was of that Thing, *La Cosa Nostra*, This Thing of Ours—or what was left of it—one of the few to survive the Executioner's long one-man war that all but annihilated the Mafia within the borders of the United States. His name was Samuel "Sammy the Shoe" Tresa, so called because a congenital defect required him to wear a built-up orthopedic shoe on his right foot.

Bolan glanced down again at the limp bundle of clothes by his feet that had just lately been a man. He was not Mafioso; that Bolan was almost certain of. During his years of constant conflict with that cancerous growth on the corpus of society, the Executioner had built up a mental mug file of thousands of made men, those admitted to that unholy brotherhood. As Bolan had decimated the mob, the number of snapshots in the mug file had, of course, decreased. The dead gunman was not among the ones that remained. But he had certainly come under the influence of some tough company.

Sam Tresa was one of the worst, a cheap hood who had never risen much above Mafia soldier because he was too innately vicious to have any real brains. Bolan had last seen Sammy the Shoe on that Terrible Tuesday of his final six-day blitz, which had mopped up the remnants of the Mafia like so much greasy gravy. The California Concept, the Mob plan to infiltrate the highest levels of major corporations, even of governments—to, in fact, form an invisible second government within the richest and most powerful nation in the world—this had brought Bolan to Southern California on the second day of that second mile.

That day had ended on a bluff above a beach house perched in Pacific Palisades, when Bolan sent a blazing message of death to the three men behind the scheme. Sammy the Shoe was head cock, or security chief of that house. He was ineffectually patrolling the beach below while Bolan visited hellfire upon it from above.

Tresa's hideously scarred face was a testament to the fact that he had not entirely escaped Bolan's firestorm.

The car was pulling away from the curb and gathering speed. It had never even come to a full stop. But that was no comfort. That Caddy was full, and this was no recon mission.

They'd be back, and Bolan guessed soon. They had to figure that their advance man had swept the area, and now they were coming in for the hit.

Only there was going to be a little something in their way.

Bolan clicked the selector switch. Adamian was still talking. He seemed to be answering a question about the aims and purposes of his Armenian Union. It would all be down on the tape for dissection later.

Right now Mack Bolan had other fish to fry.

It was time to go extravehicular again.

Sure. It was time to go hard.

2

Mack Bolan could not honestly say that he welcomed the respites between missions. In point of fact, they made him uneasy. It was not that he missed the action.

What Bolan felt was impatience, the unslakable urge to get on with a job that had to be done. There were too many arenas of conflict in the world—arenas created by man, with his rapacious instinct for the repression of his fellow man—that demanded Bolan's special skills.

He had welcomed the trip to L.A. His personal store of intelligence on the rampant upsurge in international terrorism was always growing, and he embraced any chance to supplement that knowledge firsthand. It was also an opportunity to check in with Gadgets, Pol, and ex-L.A. cop Carl Lyons: old friends, fellow warriors against Animal Man, wherever he dared to rear his head. The three formed his Able Team, based here in L.A.

Finally, Bolan trusted Hal Brognola's judgment almost as much as his own. The top cop had had a hunch that this one could be bigger than either of them suspected.

And he had damn sure been right....

Bolan was dressed in the black nightsuit that fit him like a second skin. The 9mm Beretta Brigadier, the Belle, was snug in its snap-draw holster under his left arm; the thundering .44 AutoMag hung from military webbing at his chest. Spare magazines for both were clipped to his chest, within easy reach. Bolan secured the van and stepped out into the night, his night.

And came face to face with the actor he had seen on the front lawn of the party house twenty minutes earlier.

If the man had been weaving before, he was staggering now. He looked blearily at Bolan.

"Come on," he said, his slurred voice barely understandable. "You're mishin' the party. Lotsha girlsh...."

The actor took one step forward and passed out in Bolan's arms. That was just what he needed. Bolan dragged him to the car parked in front of the van, a low-slung '57 T-Bird in what looked like mint condition. The top was down. Bolan draped the man across the bucket seats and crossed the street.

Bolan had been EVA within forty seconds of the Caddy's surveillance pass, but the drunken actor had cost him some numbers. If Bolan were right, the Caddy would be back within moments. That's when the numbers would zero out.

The Adamian mansion was surrounded on three sides by a high thicket, half hiding a redwood fence. That dictated a frontal assault, and they had numbers, weapons, and experience. Sammy the Shoe had enough brains to assure that part, at least.

Bolan cut across the street, running low, and gained the shadows of the palms. He paused for a moment, then started up the sloping lawn at a dog trot.

An overhead fixture in the portico threw a watery circle of light onto the lawn in front of the house. Under it, the chauffeur from the Rolls-Royce was working on another cigarette, his back to Bolan.

Bolan had just reached the edge of the pool of light. That put him within twenty meters of the portico, and that was his position when the Caddy came screaming down Benedict Canyon Drive and wheeled hard into the driveway.

Bolan dropped flat to the ground. Out of the corner of his eye, he saw the chauffeur turn in surprise to gawk at the long black car careering up the drive. The cigarette fell from between his lips.

The big silver AutoMag was in Bolan's right hand, extended and supported at the wrist by his left, in firing-range position. He tracked onto the front of the car, held for a split second, then squeezed.

The first round tore into the left front fender and plowed on into the engine block. The second round followed like an echo, shattering the window on the driver's side and sending 240 grains of smoking death into the man behind it.

Another man screamed in pain, a high wail. The big Caddy careered off the drive and cut a furrow in the well-manicured lawn.

The doors of the Caddy burst open, and seven men scrambled out. The dome light revealed the eighth, the driver. He was slumped over the wheel, and the side of his head was a ghastly mess of red and white and gray.

Sam Tresa came out the rear door facing Bolan and dropped to the grass. "Move it," he screamed. "Goddammit, go."

But Tresa's order didn't seem necessary to spur the men on. Despite the impact Bolan's ambush should have made, they were making straight for the house. No one except Tresa even seemed to wonder where the bullets were coming from.

Bolan snapped a shot in Tresa's direction and was rewarded by a ragged yelp of pain. But the other six did not slow their charge. The one in front carried a submachine gun, the others handguns. As they entered the circle of light, one part of Bolan's mind registered that the men were not wearing the Mafia uniform, a business suit. Instead they were dressed in blousy shirts and baggy pants, and each wore a tall pillbox hat.

The fourth slug from the AutoMag caught the

leader between the shoulder blades. He pitched forward, and the weapon skittered across the pavement into the darkness. At the same moment someone else fired, and a red stain spread across the front of the chauffeur's uniform jacket. A look of infinite surprise crossed his face, and then he slumped behind the Rolls.

The shooter was looking for another target when Bolan took the back of his head off.

The remaining four slowed for the first time. They were about twenty meters from the portico, forming with it and Bolan a roughly equilateral triangle. One of them shouted an order in a language Bolan did not recognize.

One dropped to his knee and began to return fire. A bullet plowed into the grass a few feet from Bolan's head. A second shot went high and wide, the attacker's gun arm describing a wild arc as he clutched with his other hand at his middle, where a split second before a 240-grain slug had torn a hole the size of a softball through his guts.

The other flanker dived for the discarded submachine gun. The remaining two men continued their charge, ignoring the fire behind them. Bolan came up running, holstering the AutoMag in favor of the lighter Beretta as he moved.

He was nearly on them when the numbers went straight to hell.

Adamian and two middle-aged men, all immaculate in business suits, appeared framed in the light of the open front door.

The sight of the three men whipped the attackers into a crazed frenzy. They started screaming, "*Giaour, giaour,*" almost like a chant. The faces of the three Armenians whitened.

The man who had recovered the submachine gun started to bring it up at the word of his cohorts. It was the final move of his life, as a 9mm steel-jacketed whizzer tore through him from less than ten feet away.

The last two gunmen were almost on the men at the door. Bolan cursed under his breath and tracked the Beretta onto the nearest one.

Four shots sounded so closely together that it was impossible to distinguish their separate sounds. One of the Armenians pitched back into the house at the same time Bolan's own shot crackled into the killer's head. Bolan moved his gun a few clicks to the left, but the final attacker was already punching backward toward him, until his head slammed onto the paved drive with a sickening thump.

Adamian stood stiffly erect just outside the door, alone now. There was a rough tear in his suit coat high on the left arm, already starting to ooze red. In his right hand was a .45 automatic, its big ugly black eye staring straight at Bolan's stomach.

Bolan holstered the Beretta and stepped into the full light.

"Put down the gun, Mr. Adamian," he said calmly.

Adamian stared at him, took in the black nightsuit covering Bolan's 200-pound-plus frame. His eyes swept up to meet Bolan's icy blue-eyed gaze.

He lowered the gun and said, "Who are you?"

"I'd make it about ninety seconds before the police arrive," Bolan said. "The only questions we have time for are mine. Do you know these men?"

"No."

"Why were they trying to kill you and your guests?"

"How did you know?..."

"Answer the question," Bolan interrupted, his voice sharper.

"I don't know."

Bolan knew the man was lying. Adamian winced at a stab of pain from his arm wound and looked away from Bolan's hard stare.

"They are Turks," Adamian said. "We are Armenians." Sure, Bolan thought. As if that explained it all, as if that were reason enough to explain what had suddenly turned a Beverly Hills estate into a killground.

But it would have to hold for now. The numbers were up.

"How's the arm?" Bolan said, more gently.

"It is nothing. A flesh wound is all."

Bolan allowed him a quick grin. He knew from multiple personal experiences that right now Adamian's arm would be throbbing as if someone were holding a red-hot iron to it. There was something about Adamian that appealed to the blitzing warrior; if Bolan had to make a snap judgment, it would favor the Armenian. He was a big man, as tall as Bolan, broad-shouldered and obviously a man who kept himself in good shape. He looked several years younger than the forty-eight Bolan knew him to be.

"Good night, Mr. Adamian," Bolan said, and moved toward the shadow.

He stopped at its edge and turned back for a moment. Adamian had neither moved nor taken his eyes from Bolan.

"What does *giaour* mean?" Bolan said.

" 'Infidel,' " Adamian said somberly. "In Turkish. A bad thing to call any man." He seemed to pull himself more erect. "I believe I hear sirens," he said calmly.

Bolan had already heard them, coming up quickly. But this one wasn't quite finished yet.

Bolan found Sammy the Shoe Tresa curled up in a fetal position on the grass near the crippled limousine. He was lying in a thick dark pool of his own blood. A lot of it had already flowed.

The heavy lead from the AutoMag had plowed into Tresa's left leg just below the hip and continued down to shatter his thigh bone. On the way it also severed an artery. Tresa had somehow managed to press a hand against the entry wound, and his handkerchief was stuffed into the hole where the slug had come out. Blood pumped out weakly between Tresa's fingers.

Bolan crouched in the shadowy darkness next to the dying Mafioso. The sirens got louder, and then two black-and-whites with "Beverly Hills Police Dept." stenciled in a shield on their sides tore up the driveway, their headlights sweeping over Bolan's head. He waited until they got to the portico. It would be only a matter of minutes before they got around to checking out the Caddy.

Bolan gently turned Tresa's head, and for a moment there was no expression in the man's wide eyes except pain and the knowledge of imminent death. Then the eyes went even wider, and the pain gave way for just a moment to gaping surprise.

"My God," Tresa whispered hoarsely. "Bolan. You're dead. New York, that rig of yours, they blew it sky high, right there in Central Park. Oh, my God." He closed his eyes, then opened them a moment later. "They said you were dead," he said again, hurtfully, as though somebody had broken a blood oath.

"Someone came to you, Sammy," Bolan said. His voice was very low, almost expressionless, but there was a hard edge to it at the same time. "They told you how to make contact with the Turks, and they told you what they wanted set up."

Tresa opened his mouth, struggled to get out the word. "Yes," he breathed.

"Who was it?"

Tresa shook his head. The effort took all his strength.

"You're dying, Sammy," Bolan said in that same lethally quiet voice. "You know that."

"Don't know him. Not in the Family. Never saw him. Nobody did."

"What did you call him?" Bolan pressed. "The name, Sammy."

"No name," Sammy said. "Paradine. Some kind of code or something. Just Paradine." The Mafioso nearly smiled then. The smile turned into a ghastly chuckle, and then the chuckle became a choking rattle. His eyes went glassy, and his mouth froze in a grotesque *O*.

Bolan left him and went to the street and across to the van. Incredibly, the TV actor was still passed out in the sports car, but a couple of dozen people were gathered on the front lawn of the house where the party was, staring at him.

As Bolan unlocked the van, a man called out, "Hey, wait a minute." A woman said, "You ought to make him stop," but in a bored tone, as if she were already losing interest.

Bolan swung away from the curb, passed a couple of houses, then flicked on the van's headlights.

A man was caught in the glare. He was tall and slim, with longish blond hair, and he was wearing wraparound sunglasses. The eyegear was out of place at this hour, even in Beverly Hills. As Bolan passed, the man turned his head to follow his progress.

Two more Beverly Hills P.D. cruisers tore past in the opposite lane, lights flashing and sirens whining. Bolan cut across Sunset Boulevard and through the Beverly Hills business district, then took Wilshire west to the San Diego freeway. He eased into a middle lane, then reached for the microphone clipped to the dashboard, which automatically tied into the control console's transmitter. Gadgets Schwarz answered immediately.

His eyes on the highway, the big man in black requested transport arrangements for Washington, D.C. "Immediate departure," he added.

"You got it," Gadgets said. He had obviously been monitoring the police bands, because he followed his confirmation with a barrage of coded questions.

Bolan cut him short. There were too many things he wanted to chew over in his own mind. Gadgets understood.

"Stay hard, Sarge," he signed off.

Yeah, Bolan said to himself. Stay hard.

Always.

3

Hal Brognola took a sip of his coffee, grimaced, and said, "Now I remember what I forgot to bring: a thermos of my own brew. Every time I taste this stuff you call coffee, I get the distinct feeling someone's trying to poison me."

"He likes it that way," April Rose said, nodding toward Bolan. "I'm with you. I'd rather drink kerosene."

Bolan grinned at them. Inside he was impatient to get on with the briefing, but he knew the tension they both felt, and he understood that the joking helped them to deal with it. April returned the grin. She was a tall girl, strikingly built, with flaring hips and jutting bosom, dark, silky hair, and shining eyes that turned especially luminous when she looked at Mack Bolan. She also held a degree in electronics and had done considerable graduate work in solid-state physics.

She and Mack Bolan had come together on the first day of the Executioner's last bloody mop-up of the remnants of the Mafia. She was Hal's idea; he called her a "project technician." Actually, she was to serve as liaison during Bolan's second bloody mile, and to provide back-up support. Bolan resisted; he had seen too many of his allies end up dead, or worse—as "turkeys," gory masses of technically alive flesh and screaming nerve endings, desperate for the mercy of death to end their torture.

But there had been no time for argument. And during the first few days of that final, week-long war, April became in turn associate, ally, and then true and large friend. Now, as "housekeeper" of Mack Bolan's Stony Man Farm base, she was responsible for every facet of day-to-day operations, including maintenance, communications, personnel deployment, and liaison with the other Stony Man teams, as well as with the feds in that wonderland on the Potomac called Washington.

The three of them were sitting in what Bolan called the "War Room." It was located adjacent to the primary command center, a converted three-story colonial farmhouse.

The farm featured the most modern facilities, carefully camouflaged to provide a secure retreat and working base for Mack Bolan and his teams. The 160-acre spread had been a working farm for most of its 200-year existence, and some of the fields were already plowed and would soon be planted with crops. Close to the big house were various outbuildings, all of which had been converted to serve the base's needs. The dairy barn doubled as armory and base supply. The hay barn could billet up to 200 troops, and there were less austere VIP quarters on the upper level. A gymnasium, theater, and athletic fields were available to the personnel. The garage housed the farm's motor pool, while the communications facilities had ComSat capability and a direct computer tie to Washington. All this was secured by an electrified fence, remote servo-controlled surveillance cameras, and a sophisticated electronic vehicle/personnel identification system.

The farm was located in the shadow of the Shenandoah Mountains in north-central Virginia, twenty minutes by air from D.C. From the front porch of the main house, Bolan could see the mountains' high ridge to the west, along which ran the Appalachian Trail. Stony Man Mountain dominated the vista, rising to just over 4,000 feet. To the south, Hawks Bill Mountain rose toward the sky. Now, with spring coming early to the area, the hills were already starting to green up, the leaves returning to the oaks and maples, the grass starting to color.

It was not long past sunup when the meeting in the War Room convened. Bolan had returned four hours earlier and grabbed a few quick hours of combat sleep, then wolfed down the chow that April had prepared before she joined the others.

The War Room was set up to facilitate just the kind of briefing that was taking place now. Several conference tables could be combined to seat as many as two dozen people, or separated for more intimate groups. Its walls featured an array of oversized video screens, as well as one for slides and film. A library of videotapes were designed to supply graphic back-up to any discussion. It included detailed maps of virtually every corner of the world, designed by National Security Council cartographers from public sources as well as from the latest field intelligence. The tape library also included photographs of tens of thousands of individuals from all over the world, an up-to-date electronic mug file of terrorists, assassins, mercenaries, and extremists.

Bolan turned and nodded a good morning to a new member of the group. This was Aaron "the Bear" Kurtzman, a large, rumpled man who usually wore a lab coat spotted with pipe ashes. Kurtzman was almost a human extension of the computer's electronic brain; of them all, he clearly had the most intimate relationship with the giant data bank. Kurtzman could take a raw request for information, organize it into the precise terms the computer responded to, and then sit back while it spewed out a veritable torrent of data and intelligence. In his private moments, Kurtzman likened himself to a composer: he arranged a diversity of input into some kind of harmony for his orchestra, the computer. The playback, the computer's cooperative production of all the information he demanded, was beautiful music to the scientist.

Now Kurtzman sat in one corner of the War Room at a control terminal tied into the main brain. His pipe clenched in his teeth, Kurtzman was busily feeding preliminary data coordinates into the machine. Although the console was only a little bigger than an office typewriter, Kurtzman could use it to address the entire tape library on a random-access basis, as well as control the visual display systems in the room.

Hal Brognola put down his coffee cup and straightened a pile of papers that was already straight. "Let me run through a little background material," he said, "and then I'll try to tie it all together for you."

He examined the top sheet for a moment. "Our country's relationship with Turkey has been uneasy for years. First, most of the heroin that found its way into the U.S. came from Turkish poppies. In 1971, Turkey agreed to halt the production of raw opium, from which heroin is refined, in exchange for $37.5 million in U.S. aid. But in 1974, Turkey violated this aid agreement by using U.S. arms to invade Cyprus, which it still holds.

"When we cut off the aid, they closed our military bases. After a lot of behind-the-scenes negotiation, we started up the aid again in 1978, and they let us reopen four bases. But that same year Turkey and the U.S.S.R. signed a nonaggression pact, and now Turkey is taking the Soviets' handouts as well as ours."

Brognola turned to the next sheet. "Turkey is currently being wracked by a wave of internal terrorism that goes back to 1975. It's politically motivated, and it's coming from both sides, the left and the right. And legitimate parties at both ends of the spectrum are believed to be giving at least tacit support to clandestine terrorist groups. It's become so bad that fifteen to twenty people *a day* are being killed. And it's not just terrorist against terrorist.

In the past two years, eight Americans have been killed, as well as several other members of the foreign and diplomatic communities."

"What brings us in at this time, Hal?" Bolan asked.

"Several things. First, the Turkish government has asked for help. The ruling conservative party and the moderate left have agreed to fight terrorism together, and they want our support. The president was reluctant to get our hand in—we all know how these involvements tend to escalate. But if they refuse our help, the Russians will be only too willing to oblige. And Turkey's Middle East location, at the eastern end of the Mediterranean, bordering on Russia, Syria, Iran, and Iraq, makes the country extremely strategic in the current world situation. The president was faced with a hell of a decision, but now it's out of our hands."

"How?" April asked.

"The Turkish terrorists, left and right, have struck an unholy alliance, with Russian backing. Apparently they're convinced that once they've got rid of the common enemy, they can fight it out among themselves. Who knows how these insane bastards' minds work? But we know one thing for damn sure—they're about to bring the battle right into our streets. Not with guns or bombs or troops, either. Not violence of the flesh, just violence of the spirit." Brognola leaned forward. "They've got a little white powder to do their fighting for them."

It was almost four in the morning, Los Angeles time. The last police officer had left a half-hour before. Marko Adamian was physically tired, but his spirit was elated. The firefight on his front lawn had frightened him, certainly. What man would not be frightened by such an experience? But it also meant that the time for action had finally come, the time Adamian had anticipated for months.

He sat in his conference room, the table before him empty except for a telephone. It was a private, unlisted line, its number known only to those committed to Adamian's cause. When it rang, Adamian lifted the receiver with a steady hand. He listened for a few moments, said "Yes," twice, and replaced the receiver. Then he went to the front of the house and turned off the light shining in the portico.

In the front closet there was a traveling bag, already packed. He took it out, placed it by a comfortable armchair, and sat waiting in the darkened room.

The big man dressed all in black both troubled and impressed Marko Adamian. It was quite possible that he owed this man his life. Yet he could not understand what the man had been doing on his front lawn, and how he had come to be there. Adamian recognized in this man something special, something he had seen in few men before. An air of quiet assurance, of strength, and of something more. That something more was an aura of goodness and right, and that was the troublesome part. Certainly that man in black meant a threat to Adamian's grand plan. But he also had sown the slightest seed of doubt in Adamian's mind, doubt that his plan was truly the course of what was right.

In some ways, the man in black reminded Adamian of another man he had met recently. Physically, this other man was somewhat different—tall also, but almost slim, blond, with eyes always shaded behind very dark glasses. This man carried with him an aura as well. But while the man in black projected strength and purity, the blond man projected pure menace, unleavened by any morality. Yet Adamian knew he needed this blond man, Paradine, and *that* was the feeling he had to trust.

He shook the thought from his mind and checked the luminous dial of his watch. When exactly fifteen minutes had passed from the moment the private phone had rung, Adamian rose, picked up the traveling bag, and went to open the front door.

At first he saw no one. Then he felt the eyes on him, and a moment later he made him out, standing a few meters away and off to the side of the door, staring at him from behind the black glasses that were like insect eyes.

"Good morning, Paradine," Adamian said.

"Let's go," the other man said curtly, in the flat, accentless voice that seemed almost to cut into Adamian.

Adamian shut the door behind him and followed the other man toward the waiting car, squaring his shoulders as he walked, determinedly putting his doubts out of his mind.

He would have to be ready. The cause deserved that at least.

4

Men had died here.

Mack Bolan could sense their presence, as if their souls had not entirely departed the wide, sloping valley of the Shenandoah, where Stony Man Farm was nestled. Warriors, kindred spirits, perhaps a hundred thousand of them, who had died through fratricides in this valley, in a war that had pitted brother against brother well over a hundred years before.

And sure, Bolan could pick up the vibrations of those wraiths who still walked the valley. Warfare was not something he liked, nor was it something he saw as a force of good. But warfare was something he understood.

Many would see no similarity between the bluecoat or the Johnny Reb of 1865 and one black-clad fighting man operating twelve decades later. The man himself knew there was no real difference at all. Sure, the battlefields changed; the tools of the trade were refined into ever more deadly variations; the ideologies behind it all became more complex, more self-justifying. But for the line soldier, none of that really made any difference.

His job stayed the same: to fight, against the fear and weariness and frustration as much as against the enemy. To endure. To try but never really to succeed in understanding the *why* of it all. Above all, to survive.

Survival. That was one thing that Mack Bolan knew well.

And, yeah, peace was something Bolan knew, too.

This was by no means paradoxical in this man, who had dedicated his life to the warrior path. Bolan's inner nature was clear as early as his days in Vietnam. It was there that he had first earned the label of the Executioner, for his ninety-seven successful assassinations of Viet Cong and other enemy targets. But in those days he was better known as "Sergeant Mercy," for the kindness he showed to the noncombatant residents of that war-torn country, often at great risk to his own hide.

Yet this man was not a do-gooder, nor a zealot, nor some kind of white knight on a snorting charger. On the contrary, Bolan's philosophy was quite simple—if a clear preference for good over evil can be called that. A younger Mack Bolan touched on this in a letter from Vietnam to his father.

"This is not a war of ideologies," Bolan wrote, "despite what the moralists back home, on both sides of the argument, seem to think. It is a war for the future of the human spirit. And if we allow that spirit to be crushed, we fail all mankind."

Mack Bolan had kept a personal journal since the age of fourteen. He later made the following entry, while awaiting this assignment at Stony Man Farm.

> The enemy in this new war is the same as it has always been, the same as it was in Southeast Asia, the same as the Cosa Nostra was on the home front. That enemy is Animal Man, whatever he calls himself, whatever his race, nationality, so-called philosophy, or politics. Neither has my mission changed. It remains to preserve the human estate, the heritage of civilization, and positive human evolution—in short, all the noblest aspirations of the human spirit.
>
> It is easy for all of us to become complacent. War has not been fought within the boundaries of this country for over a century, when men died in this very valley. Many have no firsthand

experience of the horror of man taking up arms against man. It is much easier when the fight is muddying up someone else's backyard instead of your own. It is much easier to perceive the struggle as remote, even unreal, when the war is carried on television between reruns of some situation comedy.

But there is nothing unreal about the struggle at all. It is there, and it goes on. We cannot leave it to someone else to fight it. *We* are the "someone else," those of us who understand what has gone wrong, and what is to be done about it.

What is unreal is the perception of peace, the notion that man's oppression of his fellow man is a sometimes thing that really doesn't touch us. It is illusory, like a brightly painted backdrop on a stage that hides the rotting bare boards behind it.

At this moment, in so many corners of the globe, violence and terrorism are the orders of the day. Arabs against Jews, Jews against Muslims, Muslims against Christians, Protestants against Catholics. Whites against blacks, even men against women. From South Africa to Northern Ireland, from Haiti to Cambodia, the world is soiled with violence. Whether the roots are racial, religious, economic, or utterly irrational, the results are the same: distrust blooming into fear, then turned into raw hatred that cannot but end in the sudden and senseless death of the innocent for the betterment of the vicious few.

Then we have the professional terrorists, who don't even pretend to have an ideology. They are the worst of this unholy brotherhood, brutal mercenaries for hire to anyone with the right price, willing and even eager to kill for the unholy pleasure of the act as well as for the money.

They are men with the moral sense of a poisonous snake, belly-crawling their way through life.

I will not suffer the existence of flagrant human savagery.

The world is not made *for* people. It is made *by* people. Like everyone, I have a choice: I can sit back and hope that the world does not overtake me, or I can do my best to swing that world around in the direction I choose.

"An interesting substance, heroin," Aaron Kurtzman said pensively from his console in the corner of the War Room. Bolan, Brognola, and April turned a little in their chairs to hear him better.

"I just read the most recent scientific study on it," Kurtzman went on. "It's more than addictive. It becomes a way of life. The addict's entire consciousness is taken over by his need for it, so that his reason for existence is defined by his desperate quest to ensure that he is never without it."

"A kind of slavery," Bolan said. "The worst kind, because its victim is even robbed of his ability to comprehend his situation."

Kurtzman nodded in agreement. "It really is the most efficient instrument of enslavement ever conceived. And it doesn't affect just the addict. A large and regular supply of heroin can cripple an entire society. Have no doubt, Mack. If you can't bust this new heroin pipeline, the United States will suffer serious damage."

Kurtzman raised one meaty hand and counted the points off on his fingers. "First, it is highly profitable for the sellers. The markup between the poppy farmer and the street vendor is several *thousand* percent. That means that the terrorists at one end of the pipeline and organized crime at the other end will get fat and strong from the profits. That could undo a lot of your earlier good work, Mack.

"Second, most of the user population will resort to street crime to support the habit, seriously depressing the quality of life in our urban centers.

"Third, the economy suffers, because when goods and money are stolen, the honest person pays proportionately more for everything.

"And fourth, police agencies on all levels become overburdened, and their general effectiveness is reduced. That completes the vicious circle: the original crime thus encourages subsequent crime." Kurtzman put a match to his pipe and puffed vigorously.

"It's the ultimate army of invasion," Bolan said. "No personnel or equipment to speak of, no risk or danger. Just a little white dust that can bring a country to its knees."

"Right," Brognola said. "And that's what we're facing, Mack. The coalition government's intelligence people have discovered that the terrorists have formed a cadre in eastern Turkey. They've been subsidizing the growing of opium poppies for several years, and they've set up a plant in the area for processing it into raw opium. Now they've got enough stockpiled to move. First it goes to refining factories in southern Europe, where it becomes heroin. The Italian Mafia has a hand in that part of the operation. From there," the head fed said solemnly, "the flood starts. It ends on our streets."

"Do we have an exact location on the stockpile?" Bolan asked.

"No, but we can come close," Brognola said. "Aaron, could we have the relevant sector on display, please?"

The Bear's tobacco-stained fingers danced over the console. The lights dimmed as he called up data. A moment later a map of the eastern area of Turkey came up on one of the video screens. The Armenian Soviet Socialist Republic appeared, abutting Turkey's eastern border, a mountainous, landlocked state slightly bigger than Maryland.

"The area is rugged and sparsely populated," Brognola said. "Communications facilities are limited, and a hell of a lot could go on there that no one would know much about. But we've had a few breaks. Our intelligence sources have been able to ascertain, partially through observation and partially from reports from Kurdish nomads in the area, that the Turkish terrorist group—they call themselves the Turkish Peoples' Liberation Army—has concentrated its activity in this area, the high country north of Lake Van." Brognola's pointer indicated a large, roughly triangular body of water, then moved higher on the map. "Here, north of Van and south of the Kara River, is high mountain country. There are several abandoned mines in the area, and we are pretty sure they are using one for their base. To process the raw opium, they've got to have a generator. If we send you over in a chopper equipped with heat sensors, Striker, you should be able to pinpoint them."

Brognola looked at Bolan. The big man stared back impassively. "We can't intercede in what would appear to the world as an internal matter," Brognola said. "At least not officially. For their part, the Turkish government is justifiably afraid that if they were to go in with a large force, the word would get out, whether the operation were successful or not. That would no doubt drive into a rampage the thousands of other members of the Turkish terrorist underground who are well-entrenched in both Istanbul and Ankara."

"That's where I come in," Bolan said.

"Correct. You've got to find that damn heroin cache, Striker, and you've got to see that it never finds its way out of Turkey. You'll move out immediately. We have good reason to believe that the terrorists are about to make their play."

The head fed sat down, eased back in his chair, and took in the other three. "Okay," he said. "Questions?"

"Several," Bolan said softly. "But let's start with the obvious one. I know you've determined that Adamian fits in. How, and on whose side?"

Brognola sighed, and for just that one unguarded moment, Mack Bolan could see in the man's face all the burdens that he carried on his shoulders, all the responsibility for making decisions that, if they turned sour, could change the course of the free world for the worse. Then the top cop straightened, and the light of dedication flashed back into his eyes.

"He fits, all right, Striker," Brognola said. "And what he means is trouble, pure and simple."

5

April came out onto the front porch of the farmhouse and refilled Bolan's coffee cup. He gave her an absentminded smile, and she returned a wide grin that demanded he take a longer look. Not only was she tall and strikingly built, but she carried with her a poise that made even strangers listen to what she had to say. Now that the morning sun had warmed the air, she had changed to a pair of cutoff bluejeans and a checked shirt tied halter-style under her breasts. She looked, Bolan thought, a little like Li'l Abner's girlfriend Daisy Mae, but with dark hair.

The morning briefing had broken for a while to give Bolan time to go over some background material that had come down the line from the NSC main computer. He set aside the sheaf of papers, lit a cigarette, and sipped at the coffee. He was impatient to get on with it, but there was a question in the girl's eyes that demanded an answer.

"It's starting again, isn't it?"

"It never ended," Bolan said. "You know that."

"Damn it," she said suddenly.

Bolan stood up and faced her. "What is it, pretty lady?" he asked softly.

"Nothing," she snapped. But then her voice softened too. "That's a lie," she went on. "It's a whole lot."

"I understand." And he did, perhaps more than he would ever be able to express to this woman in words.

"No," April said. "Let me get it out now, and maybe I won't have to go through this every time." She took a deep breath. "It's always going to be this way, isn't it? Somebody's after someone someplace, and *they* send you off as though you were some piece of machinery. And you go right along with it. In the meantime, I sit here wondering whether you're ever going to come back, and if you do, whether it will be in a car or in a box."

Bolan shook his head. He reached out and ran one finger tenderly down the side of her pretty face. "No one sends me anywhere. You know that; you've made the same choices I have."

"Why does it have to be alone every time?"

"You know the answer to that one, too. We're talking about one-man quick-reaction capability, and that's something I know."

"While the woman sits at home keeping house."

Bolan laughed. "You're right," he said. "None of us trust women with the really important jobs. That must be why you're my primary mission control and why you're in charge of the whole ball of wax when I'm not here. Women's work, right?"

April laughed, too, and she flushed prettily. "Mack," she said. "I'm sorry. And thanks for listening."

She turned and shook her butt at him saucily, then disappeared back into the house. Bolan stared after her thoughtfully, then went back to his reading.

Writing in his journal later, in an attempt to sort out on paper what he had learned, Mack Bolan had cause to reflect on the nature of history. If the story of mankind was centered around a series of conflicts, as it appeared to be, it would seem to be impossible for the historian not to take sides. And yet the world was, and always had been, colored with varying shades of victory and defeat, of good and evil.

The history of the conflict between Turks and Armenians, the conflict that motivated Marko

Adamian, was rich in these subtle shadings. And it was a conflict that was as old as three millenia, and as new as the Beverly Hills firefight of the night before.

Ancient legend, Bolan learned from the NSC printout, traces the Armenian lineage directly from Japheth, one of Noah's three sons. According to this tradition, Haik, a descendant of Japheth, rebelled against Belus, an Assyrian tyrant, after the destruction of the Tower of Babel, and then fled north with his family to the area around Mount Ararat, where biblical tradition has Noah landing his ark, and where, in fact, pieces of what appear to be driftwood have been found at nearly 17,000 feet, well above tree line. The legend of Armenia's beginning has basis in fact, as well: the ancient country that was to become Armenia was called Urartu, or "land of Ararat."

Near the end of the seventh century before the birth of Christ, Urartu was conquered by the Armenians, who came in from the east and took over what was to become the Armenian homeland for the next 2,700 years. This is an area in what is now eastern Turkey, dominated by Mount Ararat on the far eastern Turkish-Russian border. The topography of this mountain country reminds some people of the American West.

The Armenian nation enjoyed a fairly stable period for most of the next 1,000 years. It developed a national alphabet, enjoyed a more or less uneasy peace with its two powerful neighbors, Rome and Parthia, and made significant cultural advances.

The turning point came around the year 300 A.D. Since the time of the apostles, Christianity had been practiced in Armenia, although it was officially repressed. But in 300, the Armenian ruler Tiridates III was converted by St. Gregory the Illuminator. A form of Catholicism called Gregorianism became the state religion, and remains the religion of most Armenians to this day.

But Tiridates's conversion was to have vast repercussions. At least one historian states flatly that it determined the course of Armenia's subsequent history.

Mack Bolan knew that throughout history, religious differences have always provided a handy excuse for man to take up arms against his brother. The first to attack Armenia's small island of Christianity was a Persian ruler named Yazdegerd II. He was so taken with his mystic Zoroastrian faith that he tried to impose it on the Armenians and attacked them when they balked. The Armenians somehow managed to prevail against the stronger Persian forces, in the process becoming the first nation in world history to go to war to defend the Christian faith.

The Armenians were not as fortunate the next time around, during the eleventh century. It was at that time that the Turks first arrived on the scene. It was the beginning of nearly 1,000 years of conflict between the two nations.

It would culminate in the most fanatical attempt at genocide in the history of the world up to that time, a concerted effort by the Turks to drive the Armenians from the face of the earth.

It was an effort that nearly succeeded. And it resulted in a deep-rooted and lasting enmity between the Turkish and Armenian peoples.

Bolan leaned back in his chair and lit another cigarette. He thought again about Marko Adamian. There was something in the man that Bolan found admirable, despite the fact that he had spent no more than ninety seconds with the big Armenian-American. It was in the way the man held himself, in the way he stood calmly to return fire as the fanatical Turks charged toward him. It spoke to Bolan, saying, *This person is good and strong; this person has chosen the path of large life.* Perhaps, too, it lay in the fact that Mack Bolan also knew the meaning of a crusade.

But Bolan also knew that there was an important difference between himself and Adamian. Bolan was fighting against a clear and present danger. Marko Adamian was nursing a grudge that went back seventy years, and about which nothing could now be done.

Bolan was fighting for justice. Adamian was fighting for vengeance.

Bolan turned back to his reading.

At its height in the late seventeenth century, the Turkish Ottoman Empire controlled the eastern two-thirds of the Mediterranean coast, as well as most of southeastern Europe and northern Africa, including Egypt. When the empire was whittled back to Turkey's present size, there was a resentment toward anyone the Turks considered outsiders, or invaders. They had considered the Armenians as such for 2,000 years. In addition, the Muslim Turks considered the Christian Armenians infidel betrayers of Islam.

The intolerance came to a head when the Turks, with a fervor born of nationalism and internal politics, decided to systematically annihilate the Armenians. The holocaust came in 1915, when 1.75 million Armenians were driven from their traditional eastern Turkey homeland into the Syrian desert. Six hundred thousand were either executed by Turkish troops, or perished during the forced march. In 1885, there were 5 million Armenians in the world. In 1920, that number had dropped to 3 million. That was something not easily forgotten by Adamian and his people, even three generations later.

"And now an Armenian faction has joined the terrorist parade." Bolan looked up to see Hal Brognola standing over his chair.

"Almost done," Bolan said.

"Good. The kicker is a group calling itself the Secret Liberation Army of Armenia, known as the SALA. They've been involved in ten terrorist attacks over the past five years. They've assassinated Turkish diplomats in Athens and Paris, and they killed the wife of the Turkish ambassador to Spain. In their last sortie, two of their gunmen shot up the Turkish Consulate in Lyons, France."

Bolan closed the folder from which he had been reading, and stood up. "It's one hell of a can of worms, Hal."

"It's that, Striker," the big fed said. "It's definitely that."

6

Incoming, Hal," Aaron Kurtzman said. A high-speed printer next to his War Room control console began to spew out copy. The others waited expectantly.

Kurtzman tore off the message and brought it to Brognola, who scanned it, scowled, and dropped it on the table in front of Bolan. April came over to read over his shoulder.

```
***URGENT***
SCRAMBLE VIA NSC
FROM ABLE/LOSA 030702P
TO PHOENIX/STONYMAN***IMMEDIATE
ATTENTION***
BT
LYONS SENDS X MARKO ADAMIAN
APPARENTLY DEPARTED LOSA AREA LATE
LAST NIGHT OR EARLY THIS MORNING X
DESTINATION AND PURPOSE UNKNOWN X
FAMILY UNCOOPERATIVE AND
APPARENTLY UNCONCERNED BUT LINK TO
RECENT INCIDENT SEEMS INDICATED X
INVESTIGATING
EOM
```

"It's starting to cook, Striker," Brognola said grimly.

"Let's have the rest of what we know about Adamian's tie-in," Bolan said.

"You've got it," Brognola said. He turned to his ever-present sheaf of papers and scanned the top sheet. "I told you on the radio link to Beverly Hills that the same name had cropped up in regard to both the Turkish terrorist heroin scheme and Marko Adamian. The name is Paradine."

"He was Sammy the Shoe Tresa's contact on the attempted Adamian hit, Hal," Bolan said. "I got that from Tresa before he died."

"We figured that, Striker. You'll see why."

"Do we have a file photo of Paradine?"

"I already checked," Kurtzman said, his fingers dancing over the keys of his console as he spoke. "No photo, but a description. I'll give it to you verbatim; there's not much to it: 'Subject six feet, two inches; weight approx. one-eighty; slim build. Straight blond hair worn over the ears; always observed wearing dark glasses, including at night. Long, slim fingers, fluid movements, regular facial features, no known identifying scars. Age: unknown, believed approx. thirty-five. Known to speak English, Russian, French; believed to speak other languages. Passport: unknown. Country of birth: unknown. Citizenship: unknown. No fingerprints on file.'"

"I saw him, Hal," Bolan said quietly. "When I left Adamian's house, a man of that description was walking toward it, a block or so away."

"That fits," Brognola said. "Okay, here's the poop on Paradine, which incidentally may be some sort of code name. He's just started to pop up recently, in all the wrong places. The man is a free-lance. Tailor-made terrorism, altered to fit anyone's needs. The hot, new profession of the eighties," he said bitterly.

"I told you there was a KGB link to the TPLA. That link is Paradine. He's working under contract to the Russian spy-guys, supposedly advising the Turkish terrorists, actually making sure they do just what Moscow wants them to. And that way, if things get messy, the fine name of the KGB doesn't get dragged through the mud."

Bolan smiled grimly. Already his mind was starting to rearrange the pieces, and he didn't like the picture that was forming.

"Follow me on this now," Hal went on. "Paradine, always open to a way to make a couple more dollars of blood money, has plenty of contacts out. One is the SALA, the Armenian terrorist group. The SALA people tell Paradine about Adamian and his World Armenian Congress, which up to now is just a fund-raising outfit devoted to Armenian nationalism. But as Paradine learns, Adamian is fervently devoted to the cause, so much so that he is ripe for making a foolish move. And Paradine forces him into one."

Brognola leaned forward, placed both hands flat on the table, and took in each one of them in turn.

"The son of a bitch sold Adamian a private army," he announced.

"What would Adamian do with a private army?" asked April.

"A symbolic strike against the Turks in the part of eastern Turkey that used to be Armenia," Bolan suggested. "A way to draw attention to his cause. A chance to be a martyr. Any one or all of those. Remember, Adamian is a man driven by his heritage."

"I agree," Brognola said. "But there's a joker in the deck. A man named Richard V. Hagen."

"Got him," Kurtzman said immediately. A picture of a well-groomed, distinguished-looking man in his late forties flashed on a display screen.

"Hagen was born Dikran Hagopian in Istanbul. His parents emigrated when he was a baby. He changed his name legally when he went to law school, and he has no history of Armenian activism. In fact, few people know of his Armenian lineage."

"He looks familiar," April said.

"You've seen him in the newspaper or on TV. Hagen was a special presidential advisor in the last administration. Then he became a private consultant. His specialty is expediting foreign trade deals for private companies. Including deals with Turkey.

"We have no evidence that Hagen isn't on the up and up," Brognola went on. "But we keep half an eye on all of these guys who deal in foreign trade. That's how we know that Hagen fits into this."

"In what way?"

"Paradine did not approach Adamian directly. He used Hagen as a go-between. This was to make the deal look more legit. Adamian was an exporter; Hagen was an expediter of export deals; and Paradine was involved in, shall we say, foreign trade. It's all as cozy as can be."

"Then the attack on Adamian in Beverly Hills was a setup," April put in.

"No," Bolan said. Brognola looked at him with an interested expression. "Adamian was supposed to die, all right," Bolan went on. "It fits in just right with Paradine's master plan to promote the Soviet cause at our expense. If Adamian is killed in his home, all hell breaks loose. It was carefully designed to look like a Turkish-Armenian terrorist clash, so it would form an additional smoke screen to obscure the heroin operation. Armenian terrorism would increase in retaliation for the 'heroic' Marko Adamian's tragic death, and terrorism is what these animals thrive on. The U.S. would suffer a serious diplomatic setback, because they would have left enough evidence behind to make it look like an American citizen was trying to start a private war on Turkish soil. And Turkish-Armenian tensions would increase, in Turkey and in the U.S. Anything that hurts us helps Paradine and the KGB."

"You've got it, Striker," Brognola said. "And there's another reason too: the revelation of Adamian's plans for an 'unprovoked' attack in Turkey would probably throw that country to the Russians."

"But Adamian didn't die in that attack," Kurtzman pointed out.

"And Paradine would have had a fall-back plan," Brognola mused.

"He did," Bolan said. "Remember, there's no reason for Adamian to associate the attack with Paradine. He'd assume that the Turks were simply attacking him out of long-standing hatred because he was raising money for the Armenian cause. I think that right after the police left, Paradine—remember I saw him lurking in the neighborhood—Paradine went to Adamian, told him the plan was on and the time was now. That's why Mrs. Adamian wasn't alarmed at his absence. They had both been waiting for this to come for some time."

"Of course," Brognola said, nodding slowly as comprehension lit his face. "Adamian remains just as valuable to Paradine and the Russians as he did before, and for the same reasons."

"Find Paradine and you've got Adamian too," Bolan said. "As long as Adamian remains alive."

Brognola stood up, his face an angry mask. During his long professional life, he had seen every conceivable way man could exploit his fellow man for his own narrow purposes. There was no violence, no perversion he had not witnessed. And in all that time, and in all the years ahead of him, he knew that there would never be any getting used to it.

But Brognola knew that it was best that way. The day he did begin to get used to it, he would be no better than the other bastards.

"Okay, Striker," he said. "The mission is the same. Find that heroin cache and hit it. Hit it hard enough so that it won't get up again, ever. With this Adamian business, the country could really come up with egg on its face. But that heroin flood means walking death for tens of thousands of American citizens, and when it comes to national prestige or innocent human lives, the lives take top priority."

Bolan nodded impassively.

"But keep an eye out for Adamian too," Brognola went on. "If Paradine does have him, and if he uses him as we know he will, the repercussions won't die down for years."

Brognola extended a hand, and Bolan took it. April stared at them, her eyes moist. For a moment the two men, who had lived through so much together, stood there in that darkened room, and for that moment they stood as close as brothers.

"Don't let it happen, Mack," Brognola said.

7

Richard V. Hagen could not sleep.

Downstairs in his elegant home in the Washington suburb of Georgetown, he could hear the grandfather clock, an antique, softly chiming four o'clock in the morning. In their upstairs bedroom, his wife Ella lay next to him, one outstretched hand unconsciously draped across his chest. No sound came from the children's bedroom down the hall.

Hagen could feel the fatigue in his body, but his mind would not release two images that kept him awake. Images of two men.

One of them Hagen had met, but only once. He was a tall, slim blond man, who had called for an appointment, and he had used the names of other men Hagen knew as references. The names used required that the appointment be granted. The man had slipped fluidly into the comfortable chair across from Hagen's desk and stared at him expressionlessly through dark glasses.

Nothing this man asked was either suspicious or out of the ordinary in Hagen's profession. He wanted to make contact with a businessman named Adamian, whom Hagen knew very slightly, for the purpose of proposing a business arrangement. He agreed to Hagen's usual commission, and payment had duly arrived, in the form of a cashier's check drawn on a major New York bank. Everything was strictly aboveboard, and there was no logical reason for Hagen to feel anything but satisfaction at a job well done.

So okay, Hagen thought, why be logical? Because he most certainly did feel something else, a vague uneasiness that centered on the man's image in his mind. There was something about the man, some aura of malevolence, barely suppressed violence, and utterly calm control of the situation. And when the discussion had ended and Hagen stood and offered his hand, the blond man looked down at it with what seemed like contempt, and when he took it, the blond man's hand felt cold as death.

Hagen had never seen the blond man again. Yet Hagen had learned to heed his own intuition, and now that intuition told him he would see this man again, and the evil this man projected would descend on Hagen's head.

It was ridiculous. He knew that. And yet somehow that handshake seemed to seal a bargain with the devil himself.

Richard V. Hagen felt like a man who had bartered his soul.

The other image in Hagen's mind was vaguer, because it was of a man he had never met. Yet he could picture him well enough. This man was also tall, but broad-shouldered and full of strength. And dark. That was the part that permeated the image. Dark hair, and dark clothes all over, as if he were a part of the night through which he stalked.

In his years of public service, Hagen had made many contacts. One of them was able to find a witness to what really happened at Marko Adamian's that night, a television actor who was partying across the street. The man was drunk, and his description of the scene and that big man in black who had walked through it, visiting hellfire on the men who tried to attack Adamian, sounded like an advanced case of the D.T.'s. But as clearly as his instinct had perceived the nature of the blond man, Hagen felt in his heart that the dark man was all he was described as.

Hagen thanked God that this man, whoever he was, worked on the side of right.

That was his last thought before a voice broke through his musings.

The voice was quiet, deep, and commanding, almost hypnotic as it brought him up out of his thoughts into full consciousness that something very bad had invaded his home.

"Turn on the light on the bedstand, please, Mr. Hagen."

He did as he was told.

The man stood near the foot of the bed. His face was hidden in the shadows, but the hand holding the ugly black automatic pistol was lit by the reading lamp near the bed. It was as if the man had known just how to position himself.

Ella Hagen rolled over, blinked in the light, and then saw the gun. She opened her mouth wide, put the back of her hand to it, but did not make a sound.

"Very good, Mrs. Hagen," the man said in that carefully modulated voice. "Please don't change your mind and scream. I just looked in on the children, and they're both sleeping soundly."

"What do you want?" Hagen said steadily. He was frightened, but he was also embarrassed, sitting there bare-chested in bed with his wife while some stranger he couldn't even see stared down at him. That made him angry, and he let the anger rise and started to say something else. But the man's deadly calm tone cut him off.

"That's what I'm here to tell you, Mr. Hagen," the man said. "I'd like you to listen as if your life depended on it, because, of course, it does. And I would like you to refrain from asking any questions."

Hagen noticed that although the man's English was perfect, he spoke with the trace of a guttural, unidentifiable accent.

"There is a Pan-Am flight leaving Dulles Airport

this morning at seven-twenty-two, arriving in Istanbul via London at about two o'clock tomorrow morning, local time. You are to be on it." The man's left hand appeared with a paper folder bearing the airline's logo. He tossed the ticket on the bed at Hagen's feet.

"At the airport in Istanbul," the man continued, "you are to go to the counter of the Jet Charter Service. A private plane has been reserved in your name, and the pilot has destination instructions. You are not to ask him any questions. This flight will be met, and you will continue to follow any orders given to you. I am confident all of this is clear."

The gun shifted slightly, so Ella Hagen was able to stare into its muzzle. "For your part, Mrs. Hagen, you and the children are not to leave the house for seventy-two hours. You are not to initiate any outside contacts, except to cancel any appointments you may have. You and the children have contracted the 'bug' that is going around. The doctor has told you that it is highly contagious but not serious, and that you are to stay in bed for several days. Luckily, your husband had to leave town unexpectedly on business and missed coming down with it."

Ella Hagen closed her mouth and nodded.

"Should either of you fail to do exactly as I say—and I assure you, you are both under surveillance—you, as well as your children, will be killed. Have no doubt that it can be done as easily as I am standing here." The man chuckled, an eerie, disembodied sound. "You can bet your life on it," he added.

The man took two steps backward, and the shadows swallowed him.

Ella Hagen began to sob and clutched desperately at her husband. He took her in his arms and stroked the back of her head, but his mind was not on solace.

One part of him was scared, as scared as he had ever been. But the other part of him was overcome by an eerie calm. Somehow the dreadful anticipation had been banished; now it had started for real.

And then the chill overtook him, and his whole body began to tremble.

Because Richard V. Hagen suddenly knew for a certainty that the uneasy feelings of his mental images could not touch the horror of the reality on which he was about to embark.

Mack Bolan stood on the porch of the Stony Man farmhouse and ran it all through his mind once more.

And yeah, it was plenty to digest, all right.

It was the kind of story Mack Bolan had heard more and more often since beginning this third mile of his long battle march. He knew he would hear it again.

It involved two kinds of men. One kind, like Marko Adamian, was basically good and moral, but his moral vision had become too narrow. This kind wore the blinders of his own biases, and because of this he became ripe fruit for the other kind to feed upon.

Another kind of man, yeah. A man who would use anyone or anything, use them in the most vicious ways, do anything to further his godless goals.

Goals like subjugation, repression and, ultimately, domination.

Goals he could not be allowed to realize. Could not, and *would* not.

Bolan flexed his shoulder and neck muscles and realized he had been holding his body tense and rigid as these thoughts passed through his mind. To his right, a chopper approached, preparing to land on a section of recently plowed land near where he stood.

April came out on the porch and stood quietly to one side as the big Army chopper descended and settled awkwardly onto the grass. The pilot, buglike behind the tinted face-plate of his helmet, gave a thumbs-up and waited with the rotors turning.

"Mack," she said softly. She brushed his arm with her hand, very lightly. The big man looked down into her open lovely face, saw the words in her gaze, and replied in kind.

Aaron Kurtzman came out of the big house and stood to one side diffidently, until he caught the big man's eye. Bolan smiled at April. She took a step toward him, but then she seemed to make herself turn, and went into the house.

Bolan took the piece of yellow paper Kurtzman proffered. It was a teletype message logged a few minutes earlier.

```
***OPERATIONAL IMMEDIATE***
CODE TWO
FROM NSC/WASHDC 041600E
TO
PHOENIX/STONYMAN***IMMEDIATE***
BT
BROGNOLA SENDS X RICHARD V HAGEN
OBSERVED DEPARTING ISTANBUL LATE
YESTERDAY VIA PRIVATE CHARTER X
FLIGHT FILED FOR AGRI FAR EAST
TURKEY BUT NO ARRIVAL RECORDED X
PRELIMINARY REPORT INDICATES HAGEN
AIRCRAFT DEVIATED INTO RUSSIAN
AIRSPACE X REPORT NOT YET CONFIRMED
X TURKISH AUTHORITIES OFFICIALLY
REGARD AIRCRAFT AS MISSING AND DOWN
SOMEWHERE ALONG FILED FLIGHT PATH X
OUR ISTANBUL SECTION INVESTIGATING
ASSUMING LINK TO ADAMIAN AND TPLA
DRUG ACTIVITIES X NO CHANGE REPEAT
NO CHANGE IN STONYMAN PRIMARY
MISSION OBJECTIVES
EOM
```

Bolan handed the paper back to the waiting Kurtzman.

"One more piece falling into place in the big picture," the Bear said. "Good luck, man."

Mack Bolan knew luck would have nothing to do with it.

There was a family reunion set for eastern Turkey. Marko Adamian, the man called Paradine, some Turkish terrorists who planned to use a heroin flood as their stepstone to revolution, and now Richard V. Hagen, expediter, former presidential advisor, and man about the world.

Mack Bolan started toward the chopper.

It was time for one more guest to join the party.

8

His hands moved over the combat rigging, taking inventory, checking position. On his hip, the big .44 AutoMag, three and one-half pounds of screaming silvered fury. Under his left arm in shoulder-leather, the silenced Beretta Brigadier, primed to deliver whispering death. Twin stilettos in swiveled sheaths on the utility belt, tempered steel honed to razor-sharpness, and next to them wire garrotes crossed and ready for the double flick of the wrist that would bury them in the flesh of a man's neck. Leg and chest pouches held smoke and frag grenades, the drifting cloak of invisibility of the one to be blasted wide open by the flesh-shredding crash of the other.

His body was sheathed in skin-tight black fabric, and he walked silent as fog on soft-soled black footgear. A black cosmetic covered his face and hands.

The Executioner stepped into the night and became a part of it.

The Georgetown house sat alone, dark and massive except where garish electric light provided harsh contrast in the windows. A stone wall surrounded it. There was a guardhouse at the single gate.

The terrorist who had taken over the guardhouse did not see Mack Bolan until the stalking warrior opened the door to his little cubicle, and then he did a stupid thing. He tried to reach for an alarm button with one hand and for the autorifle on the table next to it with the other.

He had completed neither movement when a Bolan 9mm Parabellum punched into his face.

Mack Bolan moved across the elegant expanse of lawn, the night embracing him like a long-lost relative. Two hardmen stood near the front door of the Hagen residence, profiled in the spill-light of a front window.

"Hey there," Mack Bolan said softly.

One man was holding a match in hands cupped against the breeze, and the other had a cigarette in his mouth, and his head ducked toward the flame. Neither even bothered to look up.

"That you, Sid?" the smoker said around his butt. "You're a little late, but I guess there's some left for you. I was first in line for her."

"Good for you," Bolan said, and shot the man in the side of the head.

The other guy dropped the match and clawed desperately under his arm. He never even came close. His fingers were just scraping the butt of his handgun when the Belle sneezed and a steel-jacketed slug punched through his skull as if it were a ripe melon.

Two more men were staring mindlessly at some TV cartoon in the front room, with plates and sandwiches in their laps. One was raising his sandwich to take a bite when Bolan said, "Over here," in the flat, toneless voice of death. The man turned and stared, and his mouth was still gaping open when he swallowed a tumbling bite of eternity. His pal dived toward a sofa, where a submachine gun lay propped against the cushions, and Bolan helped the guy along with a whizzer through the neck. On the TV, a duck beat on a pig with a baseball bat.

Footsteps pounded on stairs, and a moment later an armed man appeared at the door in time to catch a burst from the chattergun that ripped him from crotch to shoulders and slammed him into the man behind him. The autorifle spoke again, and then a third time, and other men collapsed in the mess of their comrades. And then they stopped coming.

Bolan went up the stairs and crossed a hall. Light

came from behind a door, and Bolan pushed it open and went in.

A man sat behind a desk. He wore a business suit, and he was impossibly fat. Rings on both hands were buried in the soft white flesh of his fingers. Rolls of blubber like inner tubes ringed his neck about his collar. His lips were thick and greasy, and he stared at Bolan from tiny eyes set deep in the bloated meat that was his face.

He picked a smoking cigar from an ashtray on the desk and held it between two sausagelike fingers.

"I think you've made a mistake," he said, in a curious, high-pitched voice.

Bolan leveled the AutoMag and fired from three meters away.

There was a mangled stump of wrist where the man's hand had held the cigar. The man stared at it and fainted. Blood spurted out and washed across the polished desktop.

Bolan left the room and closed the door behind him.

Another door, this one at the very end of the hall, stood open. Beyond it was darkness. Bolan took a step toward it.

From the darkness came a sound.

It could have been the mewling of a wounded animal, knowing life was over, crying for the mercy of death.

Mack Bolan knew it was the sound of a human being.

He turned his back and faced the stairs leading away from there and down into the night. He let out his breath and lowered the gun in his hand, but he did not move toward those stairs.

And finally, with no sense of thought or decision but only the certain knowledge that there was only one direction he could take, only one path he could walk, Mack Bolan turned again and moved toward the dark room, and Mrs. Hagen.

"We'll be landing at Sao Miguel, the Azores, in ten minutes, Colonel Phoenix," the young lieutenant said respectfully. "About a half-hour layover, if you want to stretch your legs."

"Thanks," Bolan said. "I'll take you up on that."

He turned to look out the window of the aircraft. False dawn faintly lit the eastern horizon, and he could see the choppy waters of the Atlantic below as the plane started its descent.

He sat up straighter in the seat and pulled the lap-belt tight. Bolan had long ago learned how to take advantage of a brief respite to catch some combat sleep, his body rejuvenating in deep relaxation, his mind on the edge of alertness and ready to snap to the moment it was necessary.

But no, what had come to him was not a dream. It was a vision, a vision of what had come so many times before, and what would most surely come again. The woman his consciousness knew was in the room at the end of the hall—and now Bolan deliberately put from his mind the thoughts of those who had died horrifying deaths in aid of his cause. That woman represented something greater than one person. She stood for the ones who could not stand on their own against the onslaught of terror and senseless violence. Not because they were weak, not because they did not have the courage.

But because they had not been trained in the same savage skills that the enemy had honed to a profane art.

Mack Bolan knew those ancient warrior skills. Knew them, and knew how to fling them back in the faces of those who would seek to prey on the weak. And he knew the responsibility his knowledge required of him.

So yeah, there was only one path Mack Bolan could walk, and walk it he would, without turning back. If there was momentary hesitation, it was a sign not of the man's indecision, but of his humanity.

The contemplation, the questioning of rightness, was what separated the hunter from his animal prey.

Once again that question had been answered, clearly and without ambiguity. And that was what Mack Bolan's vision was about.

A few minutes later, Bolan stepped out of the plane and filled his lungs with the damp sea-salt air, then exhaled slowly. A full crew scrambled around the plane, saluting him deferentially while double-timing the refueling.

Twenty-four minutes later, they were airborne again, heading due east for the Mediterranean.

9

The airstrip on which the private jet bearing Richard Hagen landed was in the middle of an isolated high-country meadow. It was unmarked and unmanned, although the tarmac was well-maintained. Almost before the hydraulic wing-door was fully raised, a hand locked around Hagen's arm, and he was pulled roughly from the compartment.

As a presidential advisor, one of Hagen's fields of specialization had been the Middle East. He was able to figure out a few things based on the knowledge gained at that time, and to make some educated guesses as well.

The guard that dragged him from the plane barked something at him. Although Hagen didn't understand it, he recognized the tongue as Turkish. The man wore a military-type uniform and a beret, similar to the official Turkish Army uniform but without insignia. Hagen was pretty certain that the weapon that was hanging from his shoulder by a webbing sling was an AK-47, a Russian-made submachine gun.

A Land Rover was waiting on the edge of the runway, its motor banging. Another man in the same uniform sat at the wheel. As they walked toward it, Hagen felt the early-morning chill of the spring mountain air.

By gesture, Hagen was ordered to climb in through the rear door of the Rover. His guard followed. The two Turks had a quick exchange, and then the Rover lurched forward.

For about an hour they drove up over a high mountain pass, their backs to the rising sun. The road was unpaved gravel. It had not been graded since the spring run-off began, and the stiff-sprung 4 x 4 clambered in and out of deep ruts and potholes. Several times Hagen was bounced out of his seat. Once he was half flung across the small rear compartment, banging against his guard's knees. The man swung his rifle around and trained it on Hagen, snapping something in Turkish. The menace was obvious. Hagen hauled himself back into the seat.

When they reached the top of the pass and Hagen got a look around, he was not surprised to see the still snow-covered peak of Mount Ararat to the southeast. It confirmed what he had already assumed: his plane had landed in Russia, somewhere in the high country of the Armenian S.S.R., to be exact, and had just now crossed the border back into Turkey. But that posed a new question: why had he been flown from Turkey into Russia, only to be smuggled back into Turkey?

There was only one logical answer, and Hagen didn't like it one bit. These Turks, somehow and for some reason, were under Russian control. Hagen had been a foreign diplomat long enough to know what that meant.

The Rover turned north, descended to a river valley, and followed it west for a while. Finally they turned back south, taking a cut-off road that switchbacked its way up into the high country again. The road became steeper, and then, after a brief stop for what Hagen assumed was identification purposes, they were passed into the compound.

Hagen looked around the small room in which he was locked, and wondered for the fiftieth time what in God's name was going on.

Even in shirtsleeves and a twenty-four-hour

growth of beard, Hagen managed to look distinguished. But his dignity was clearly starting to fray. He paced off the six steps it took him to cross the room, turned, and retraced the path in the opposite direction. He had been doing the same thing for a half-hour.

The small room was all there was to the rough wooden cabin. Against the back wall an old, dirty mattress lay on a cot, its bare springs twisted and beginning to rust. Next to it there was a wooden packing crate. In the front wall, set into the unplaned planks from which the cabin had been haphazardly fashioned, there was a door, and next to it a single window in a frame that didn't match the rest of the boards, likely salvaged from some other building.

For the third time since he had begun pacing, the tall middle-aged man went to the door and rattled it. He didn't know why; he knew it would not open, but it was something, a gesture perhaps, a sign that he had not given up and would not. Richard Hagen did not consider himself a particularly courageous man, but he knew that if there were to be any chance of his surviving this nightmare, it would depend upon his maintaining whatever control he could muster.

Above all, outwardly he had to project calmness, even bravery. Hagen knew that an animal could smell its enemy's fear.

These men, Hagen was certain, were no better than animals.

In response to his rattle, a rifle butt pounded against the outside, and a harsh voice snapped out a threat in Turkish.

The fear and rage mixed inside Hagen and boiled over like a steaming cauldron. He pounded a fist against the rough wood of the door and screamed out a string of curses, knowing the man would not understand the words but would know their universal meaning.

The door wrenched open, and the khaki-clad guard stepped in and leveled an automatic rifle on Hagen's middle. This time Hagen had no doubt of the meaning of the man's words: if he did not keep quiet, he would be killed. Hagen turned his head slowly and deliberately and spat on the floor. The guard glared at him, then stepped out and slammed the door.

Hagen slumped down on the cot, his whole body trembling from the effort the show of courage had cost him. He wondered feverishly how long he could keep it up.

No, that was not true. He did know how long. He would keep it up until it was over. He had no choice.

Hagen shook his head clear and went to the window. The compound in which he was being held looked like some sort of temporary military base. There were two long, low buildings that Hagen took to be barracks, except there were also a dozen six-man bivouac tents, as well as a couple of smaller shacks like the one in which he was being held.

The compound occupied a gently sloping natural terrace about 500 meters below the summit of the mountain. The mountain itself sloped up much more steeply to its top, so it formed almost a wall, which extended out a way on either side of the compound, in two natural flying buttresses. The result was a highly fortified safe-camp, surrounded on most of three sides by a rock wall and fronted by a fence with only one gate that was, as far as Hagen could tell, constantly under guard.

Where the mountain resumed its steeper slope, in the back wall, a mine shaft had been cut at a down-sloping angle. But Hagen had seen no mining equipment, and he expected the mine had been abandoned. He did observe four old buses parked near the adit—troop carriers, he figured—and several Jeeps, Rovers, and other rough-terrain vehicles.

Men were working on the vehicles, as well as on a good-sized diesel generator from which power lines extended to the two long buildings. In all, Hagen estimated that he had seen more than 100 troops, all dressed in the same khaki uniforms without insignia. The colors of the beret caps varied, however, probably as indicators of rank.

As if at some signal, the men suddenly stopped working and straightened. A moment later there was clearly one hell of a commotion.

Hagen rubbed at the filthy windowpane with his shirtsleeve in an attempt to get a better look. The main effect was to smear the dirt around, but he was able to clear a small spot to see through.

Someone was shouting orders, and men were moving into the area in front of the mine shafts. Each had his autorifle slung over his left shoulder. They formed into rough ranks, with a distinct lack of precision and military bearing. They were facing the gate, but from his limited angle Hagen could not see the object of their attention. He did hear the sound of a vehicle motor.

He was still peering out the window when the door to the shack burst open.

The guard came in and again covered Hagen with the rifle. Sunlight streamed into the shadowy room, and Hagen blinked in its glare. The guard stepped aside to admit another man.

Marko Adamian came into the shack. He stumbled as another guard behind him pushed him roughly in the back. He wore the same kind of khaki fatigues as the Turks, but his were smeared with dirt and torn at one knee.

There was an ugly purple bruise high on one cheek and a worm of dried blood at the corner of his mouth.

Hagen said, "Jesus Christ," and stepped toward him.

The first guard jabbed the barrel of his AK-47 into Hagen's midsection and snapped out an order. Hagen doubled up, clutching at his stomach, fighting down the rising nausea.

"What did he say?" Hagen got out.

"You should learn your native tongue, Hagopian," Adamian said dryly. He staggered to the cot and sat down heavily.

"My native tongue is English," Hagen said. "My name is Hagen. And what did the bastard say?"

"You don't want to know," Adamian said without looking up, and then went on anyway. "He said you bawl like a goat caught in a thicket. He said if you don't shut up, he will cut off your balls so you bleat like a ewe instead."

The guard nodded curtly, as if he understood. He and the other one turned and went out of the shack. Hagen heard the lock snap home behind them.

He looked at the man on the bed. Adamian was leaning back against the wall, his eyes closed, his face set grimly against the pain.

Hagen stared at him and shook his head in disbelief. It was not supposed to be like this. None of it seemed real. This man was a suave and shrewd businessman. The last time Hagen had seen the man was in his Los Angeles office.

They had both been in business suits that day, sipping sherry out of crystal goblets.

One part of him waited for Adamian to break out in a big grin and say, "Surprise, surprise. Only fooling."

Instead, the big Armenian opened his eyes and stared at Hagen weakly.

"I made a mistake, Dikran," he said quietly. "I did not see."

Hagen sat down on the cot next to him. "What is it, Adamian?" he said. "What the hell is going on? What are we doing here?"

The other man stared back, his eyes dark and lifeless.

"Tell me," Hagen demanded.

Adamian shook his head meaninglessly and continued to stare deep into the vision that only he could see.

10

"That's Lake Van coming up ahead, Colonel Phoenix." The pilot's voice was tinny and mechanical sounding over the noise of the 'copter's engine. "Ten o'clock low, sir."

Bolan/Phoenix looked over to his left and saw the shoreline approaching, and then the water of Turkey's largest lake stretching north toward the horizon. Surrounding the lake were rocky, rolling hills growing into high, rugged mountains to the north and east. Along the lake's shore there were several fair-sized towns, the biggest being Van. Bolan could just make it out, nearly dead ahead, on the eastern shore. But away from the lake there were only the *mahalle*, the tiny rural settlements of the farmers and herders who carved a difficult living out of the land, and the camps of the nomads who ventured into the high country each summer in search of pastureland.

"Any special course you'd like to set from this point, sir?" the pilot asked.

"I understand there are some mines in the mountains south of the Kara," Bolan said. "I'd like to get a look at them, if we can get in there."

"We can get just about anywhere you'd like sir," the pilot said. "But as far as I know, those mines haven't been in operation for years. Played out, I guess."

"You know where they are, then?"

"There's quite a few of them, sir. I know the general area, and the specific location of some but not all."

"The one I'm looking for will show some activity," Bolan said into his headset. "Not mining necessarily, but definitely some goings-on. Seen anything like that?"

"No, sir. But that's extremely rugged country up there, and a lot of those mines are pretty secluded. Tough to spot unless you're right on top of them. Someone could be up to just about anything up there, and they could keep it a secret for as long as they wished."

Oh yeah, son, Bolan thought, they're up to something, all right. Up to their dirty ears in a plan to unleash havoc in the streets of America.

"Let's give it a go, Captain," Bolan said out loud. "The heat sensor should help."

"Yes, sir. But its range is limited, especially if the heat source is relatively small, like some of the more portable generators. And because the mountains are so steep, you have to get a direct line-of-sight anyway for it to be effective."

The young pilot pulled up on the stick, and the 'copter heeled to its left and moved more directly north. Bolan could see the higher country coming up ahead.

"Any problems with airspace clearance?"

"No, sir," the pilot said. "We're cleared out of our base at Diyarbakir. Those boys are always taking jaunts over toward the Russian frontier, but as long as we don't show any intention of crossing into their airspace, we're fine. We can go just about anywhere we'd like."

The young captain was enjoying the outing. The weather was clear, a high-mountain spring day with air as crisp as iceberg lettuce. The bright sun still hung low on the horizon to their left. The captain didn't know who this mysterious Colonel John Phoenix was. He did know that he was some kind of VIP, and that the captain's orders called for him to give the colonel every courtesy and to obey his orders absolutely. He also knew that successful completion of this assignment could only benefit his career.

They came in out of the sun, skimmed along the Kara River for a while as the pilot got his general bearings, and then climbed up the steep canyon walls toward the mountain peaks. The captain began pointing out abandoned mine shafts, each time taking them in close, often bringing the whirlybird in to hover right in front of a mine's mouth. And each time with the same result.

Negative. No sign of activity, no reading on the heat sensor that would indicate the presence of generating equipment or any other power-driven devices.

Yet they had to be there. Unless intelligence was wrong. Bolan shook that thought away. It would not be wrong. Everything pointed to the fact that somewhere in these mountains a bunch of fanatical Turkish terrorists, united under some phony banner that screamed "freedom" while it meant "oppression," were conspiring with the Reds to breathe new life into their fanatical drive to turn American society inside out.

No. Not breathe new life. These people breathed damp, fetid death.

And it was up to Mack Bolan to see that they breathed no more.

"Suggestions, Captain?" Bolan said.

The young pilot cleared his throat uncomfortably. "Begging the colonel's pardon, sir, but I'm really not sure exactly what we're looking for."

"Sorry, Captain," Bolan said firmly but not unkindly. "You do the flying and I'll do the looking."

"Yes, sir. As to your question, sir, we don't have much choice. I'm within ten minutes of maximum range as far as fuel goes. Regulations state that we begin to return to base now." The captain glanced over at the stony-faced colonel at his side. "I'd be happy to take the colonel up again at his convenience, sir."

Bolan's mind was racing. He knew they had to turn back, and now. No matter how important the mission, Bolan had no right to involve the young captain. This was a mission for volunteers only, and though the pilot looked game, there was no room for conscripts.

The captain was already pulling back on the stick. As the chopper rose up over the crest of the range, Bolan scanned the terrain on the dim chance that they'd finally get lucky at the last moment. He considered having the pilot set him down for a footsearch, but the idea made no tactical sense. Without a vehicle or any intimate knowledge of the area, and out of radio contact with any ally, it could take him weeks, and even then he'd have no guarantee of finding the terrorist base.

By that time, the heroin pipeline would be emptying into its victims' veins.

They came up over the ridge. On this side the country was less rugged. The chopper crossed another range of lesser mountains and came out on the kind of terrain that's called a "hole" in the U.S.: a wide, flat, grassy plain surrounded by hilly mountains, probably a lake some tens of thousands of years ago, but now with only a small stream running through it.

And the stream wasn't the only thing running through.

"Take her down, Captain," Bolan said.

The captain glanced at Bolan, and then he spotted it too.

A convoy of off-road vehicles was moving along the two ruts in the grass that served as a road. They looked as though they were in a hurry.

"Shall I make a pass, sir?" the pilot asked.

Bolan muttered his assent and took the field glasses the pilot offered.

There were five rigs. A covered Land Rover led the pack, followed by two open Jeeps. What looked like a troop carrier was fourth in the line, and another Rover brought up the rear.

"Bring her up for a minute," Bolan said.

The 'copter seemed to slide to a stop, although in fact it was now tracking the convoy from 300 feet up. Bolan took a closer look through the glasses.

It was a damned funny place to run into an armed convoy, in the middle of nowhere. There wasn't a military base within several hundred miles—except for a renegade outfit that appeared on no service roster.

Yeah, damned funny. But Mack Bolan did not operate on hunches except when absolutely necessary. Hard confirmation was always preferable.

The convoy had slid to a hurried stop. Men came out of the troop carrier, and there were excited gestures at the chopper.

None of the vehicles were marked. No insignia was visible on any man's uniform.

And then Bolan got his confirmation. A man scrambled up on the back of the second Jeep and threw back a tarp.

Beneath it two rockets were mounted on rails.

Confirmation, for sure. Hard confirmation.

Especially when the man's partner started to draw a bead on them.

"Scramble," Bolan snapped. From the corner of his eye, he saw the pilot pull hard left on the stick.

At the same time the rocket rose on a tail of flame.

"High explosive artillery rocket, sir, I believe," the captain said calmly. He scanned his instruments, then looked sideways at Bolan, his expression more curious than frightened. The VIP guide was now an efficient fighting man. Bolan could sense it, and thanked his stars that Uncle still had some of these left and that he had drawn one.

"We're out of range, sir. Orders?"

"Take me down."

"Sir?"

"You heard me, Captain. Take me down just far enough away to be out of sight of them. Then return to base."

"Instructions for rendezvous, sir?" the pilot said crisply.

"No rendezvous." There was no point to it, Bolan knew, except to risk others' lives. And this one was his fight.

"Sir..."

"That's an order, Captain."

"Yes, sir."

Bolan glanced over at the younger man and saw the tight set of his jaw as he accelerated the 'bird. A moment later he pulled up and began a quick descent.

"Captain," Bolan said, "if you're thinking of heroics, forget it. This is my show. You get me down, and you get the hell home." Bolan grinned. "Or when I get back, I'll make damn sure your butt's in a sling it'll never get out of."

"Yes, sir," the pilot said seriously. Then he returned the smile. "You watch your own butt, sir," he added.

The landing skids barely brushed the top of the meadow grass, and then the chopper swept skyward again, wagging its tail once in farewell before moving off to the south.

By that time Mack Bolan was EVA and already scouting for position.

11

Mack Bolan had been a warrior for all of his adult life. His skills first surfaced, and then were honed and refined, during the dark days of Vietnam. He had brought them back with him to the home front, and in nearly forty campaigns that spanned North America and much of Europe, he proved how effective one man can be against the bloodsuckers who leeched their ill-gotten gains from their innocent fellow citizens.

In the process, this man called the Executioner had become, quite simply, the most effective single-man fighting force in the world history of combat.

Interestingly, nothing in his youth pointed directly to the man Mack Bolan was to become. Although he made an impression on the people whose paths he crossed, it was one of quiet intelligence, extraordinary athletic ability, and a natural capacity as a leader, combined with a streak of introspection that made some people use the term "loner," though not critically.

From the good people who came to know him, he gained admiration. From those who chose to oppose him, he gained respect. Mack Bolan asked no more.

"He was just a normal guy. But at the same time he was special, if that makes any sense." This from a high-school classmate who knew the man as well as anyone in those early days. For those who became his comrades in later years, after Bolan had accepted the warrior's call, it did make sense. In his needs, his desires, his hopes, his fears, in the ways he gave himself freely and truly to those needful and worthy of his attention, certainly this was a most normal man.

In his uncanny command of the skills of death—and, more importantly, in the true and moral way in which he chose to employ these skills—here, yes, this man was truly special.

His trademark had become the rapid blitz, hit and git, the furious and unexpected firestorm from hell that left his enemies reeling, broken, and whimpering, stinking with the smell of fear, while Bolan disappeared to pop up somewhere far removed, hit again, and then fade. It was guerilla warfare, pure and simple—the same kind colonial rebels used on King George's redcoat troops in New England during the American Revolution, the same kind the Cong had used on us in Southeast Asia. It followed no rules, and it did not deal in romantic notions like "fair" or "gentlemanly."

But it worked. It damn sure worked.

Yet Mack Bolan was not a wild-ass warrior. The caricature of the combat hellion—cigar stub clamped between clenched teeth in a mouth twisted into a grotesque snarl of rage, shirt hanging in rags over a sweat- and blood-smeared chest, and a vocabulary limited primarily to grunts—this image fit Bolan about as well as a silk top hat, white tie, and tails.

Bolan undertook his blitzes with a cool head and attended to every detail of preparation possible. He nursed no death wish, although he acknowledged the very real possibility of dying. But living meant victory, and victory meant the freedom to engage the enemy once more.

For this reason, the skills of the pistol, the automatic rifle, the stiletto, and the garrote were not the only ones that Bolan utilized. There were the skills of what he thought of as "intellectual combat" as well.

The man in black had learned the psychological value of surprise, infiltration, role camouflage, and counterintelligence. He learned to heed his instincts, until he developed an almost animallike sensibility of the presence of danger, and of the goodness or depravity of the person he found himself confronted with. He learned the values of patience, observation, surveillance, and planning.

Most of all, Mack Bolan had learned the value of caution.

Others might call it pessimism, a morbid propensity for expecting the worst. Mack Bolan called it preparedness.

As much as any of his other skills, it was this that got him through the next few minutes on that grassy high plain in the empty stretches of eastern Turkey.

Mack Bolan had never been there before. He did not know the other side, except that it represented a clear and present danger to all he held dear.

But he was ready. Ready, for sure. And there was most of the ball game.

Yeah, it was their home court. But they hadn't had a look at the visiting team.

Bolan was ready to show them.

He was in full combat rig.

He had discarded the blousy fatigues to reveal the skin-tight black bodysuit, made of a rip-resistant material. Practical, like the man, with no loose ends to tie him up or slow him down. It also carried a potent psychological impact. More than one guy, when faced with this dark-clad apparition that seemingly appeared from nowhere, had felt his bowels turn to jelly and his nerve head south for the winter.

The 9mm Beretta Brigadier rode its usual position of honor, shoulder-slung in snap-draw leather. The silencer threaded on the end of its stubby barrel would seem superfluous out here in the middle of mountainous nowhere, except for, again, the psychological angle. There was something distinctly unsettling when, with no pistol-crack of warning, the man next to you suddenly toppled, the top of his head chewed to bits as if he had been sandbagged by a phantom.

The big .44 AutoMag flesh-shredder rode heavy military webbing at his right hip, fully loaded, a bullet already in the chamber. From a lanyard around his neck hung an Ingram M-11 .380 autopistol with a thirty-two-shot clip.

Cradled in his arms was the M-16/203, the regular issue autorifle with 40mm grenade launcher in tandem with it below the barrel, just ahead of the magazine.

A virtual armory of munitions dangled from the utility belts that crossed his chest, or were snugly stowed within easy reach in the skinsuit's elastic pockets. These included spare clips for each of the four firearms, as well as an assortment of grenades: buckshot, flare, gas, chemical smoke, and high explosive, all of which the M-79 accepted.

As always, Bolan had approached this assignment on full alert. Before boarding the chopper, he had been wearing both handguns beneath the fatigues, and the pockets of the skinsuit had been prefilled. Behind the 'bird's seat he had carefully stowed the Ingram and the '203, along with the utility belts, stocked and ready to slip on and snap into place.

From the moment he gave the order to set 'er down, it had taken him just under fifty seconds to rig up completely.

The double tire-trail that passed for a road was about two hundred meters distant. The stream that it paralleled separated Bolan from the road, and there was a stand of cedars along its bank. As Bolan made for the tree cover, he heard the sound of the approaching convoy. A slight rise kept them out of sight for a moment. Just as Bolan reached the trees, the lead Rover appeared, barreling through the grass.

Bolan gauged the speed and distance, made a

quick mental calculation, and flattened back against the nearest tree. He pulled a green-and-gold grenade cartridge from the utility belt, fed it into the launcher, and counted off fifteen beats.

When he stepped into the open, he was off to one side of the approaching convoy, and about fifty meters from its path. But the man in the passenger seat of the lead Rover spotted Bolan as he shouldered the launcher, and from the corner of his eye Bolan saw the man's mouth drop open even as Bolan let the can fly.

The high explosive grenade ripped into the second vehicle, a troop carrier. It hit a foot or two in front of the driver's seat, and the motor was churned into a greasy pudding of mangled scrap metal. Before it could slide to a complete stop, Bolan sent a second HE round into its tail. The converted bus slewed around and was about to flop over on its side when the gas tank blew. Instead, its rear end bucked into the air. The whole bus seemed to jump and jerk like a bucking horse before coming back down hard on splayed and shattered wheels.

Men started to stream out of the shattered back of the bus, some of them badly wounded. Bolan sent thirty-two rounds of M-16 fire in their direction as a deterrent, and followed it with a smoke grenade.

Behind the veil of choking smoke, someone was shouting orders. Bolan started to advance toward the voice, ejecting and replacing the empty clip of the M-16 as he moved. The offensive was his, and he meant to keep it.

He saw the line of men before any of them saw him. Perhaps a dozen were still able to fight. Each was armed with an automatic weapon and stood about five meters from the next. They were not advancing but just standing there, looking fearfully into the smoke.

Near the lead Land Rover a man dressed like the others, but with a red beret, was shouting orders in

Turkish. This commander was ordering them to advance, and he was clearly angry that he was being ignored.

Then one of the foot soldiers spotted the black wraith appearing like a vision from the thick smoke.

The Turk started to bring up his rifle, and Bolan put a fist-sized pattern of six shots into the middle of his chest. The blitzer tracked to the next man in line and fired almost before the man was in his sights. Bits of this guy's head were still splattering through the air when Bolan cut down the third man down the line, and then a fourth.

The other members of the rapidly dwindling front were flinging themselves to the ground, weapons extended. Bolan caught one more as he dived, and the man hit the grass not in a firing posture but in the unnatural sprawl of death.

Bolan hugged the ground himself just ahead of the first burst of return fire. He dropped another can of smoke between himself and the remaining soldiers and started flanking toward the Turkish commander.

Another soldier came out of the smoke. He looked up at the sudden appearance of the big man in black, stared down the barrel of the M-16 and the gaping hole of the launcher beneath it, and seemed to recognize that he faced death incarnate.

But instead of fear, a look of weariness and resignation came over his face. Bolan realized that the man had dropped or thrown away his rifle somewhere along the line and faced him empty-handed.

The man looked up from the weapon and into those icy eyes of Bolan's and slowly, tiredly, shook his head.

Bolan lowered the barrel slightly. The soldier closed his eyes and fell heavily to his knees.

Bolan moved past the man and back into the hellground.

The second smoke grenade was starting to dissipate. To Bolan's left as he stalked forward, a Turk hardman was working furiously trying to unjam his rifle, his head down. Bolan unsheathed the Baretta and shot him once in the head, and the man slid silently to the ground.

He came out of the smoke, and not five meters away one of the few that were left looked up, his eyes suddenly deep pools of surprise and fright. Bolan gave him a quick figure-eight burst from the Ingram, and the man was no longer there.

There was a shrillness to the commander's orders now. His shout had become more of a scream, and in it there was fear and revelation.

Yeah, revelation. The grim revelation that one man was just about on the brink of taking them to hell-and-gone apart.

A two-man crew in the back of the second Jeep was trying to bring a heavy tripod-mounted machine gun around. One of the men got in the other's way and was roundly cursed.

Bolan knelt and fired the M-203.

The two men were still arguing when the HE shell plowed into the Jeep. Parts of the men flew off into nothingness. A moment later, the secondary flipped the Jeep high into the air, and then a tertiary blast of ammo engulfed the front end of the already crippled troop carrier. Voices screamed in chorus as knife-edged pieces of Jeep-shrapnel slashed through the smoke and flames.

And then there came a different kind of scream, from Bolan's left flank. Its voice was harsh, distorted with hatred, and it was flinging a word Bolan had heard before, two days earlier and most of a globe away.

Two soldiers, the last of the advance party, were bearing down on him from forty meters away. The face of each was contorted, and although each still carried his autorifle, neither stopped to use it.

The men were shouting, "*Giaour, giaour!*" spitting the epithet as if it were a lethal device.

There was nothing of the soldier left in these men. There was only the animal lust of some strange and fervent death frenzy.

Bolan raised the Ingram, but the two Turks came on, their already dark faces now red, their eyes flashing with something sick and alive.

Bolan let the machine pistol drop. He drew the big silver AutoMag, extended it, and fired twice. The gun bucked in his hand.

The men's heads snapped back almost simultaneously. Their bodies arched in the air, seemed to hang motionless for a moment, then slammed to the ground.

Bolan holstered the gun and turned to face the Turkish commander.

But apparently the one who so freely ordered his men to their deaths had no stomach left himself. His Rover was rapidly disappearing toward the horizon. Bolan could see the commander sitting stiffly in the passenger seat next to his driver.

He did not look back.

Bolan stared after the retreating Rover until it was out of sight, then walked through the death and silence toward what was left of the convoy.

12

The interior of the troop carrier was a burned-out hulk, and flames still licked along the seats. Bodies and parts of bodies littered the inside and the ground around it. On the far side Bolan saw movement.

A Turk gunner was lying on his back staring up at the man in black, his eyes huge, gaping holes. Only the pain was keeping the hardman alive. There was a gaping wound in his chest, and his left arm was severed at the shoulder.

The Turk opened his mouth. All that came out was a bright red bubble. But the plea was obvious.

Bolan drew the Beretta and put a mercy round in the side of the guy's head. The last expression on the man's face was one of relief.

The Land Rover that had brought up the rear of the convoy, behind the troop bus, was scorched by the blast, and its windshield was shattered. Otherwise it looked relatively undamaged. Bolan got in, flicked the ignition switch, and tromped on the footstarter. A futile grinding was the only response. Then, just as the battery was starting to give out, the engine growled, coughed, and then caught. Bolan backed the Rover farther from the bus and let it idle. The gas gauge indicated a half-tankful.

There was little left of the rest of the convoy. Bolan went through the wreckage quickly but methodically, and was about to go on when something caught his eye.

It was part of the discarded launching tubes from the artillery rocket the Turks had tossed at the chopper. Bolan had seen a similar tube before, during a deep penetration mission behind North Vietnamese lines. It was a single-rocket adaption of the BM 21.

And it might just as well have been stamped, "Made in Russia."

It was sure as hell not part of the arsenal of the regular Turkish armed forces, or of any other NATO country, for that matter. The only armies using this 122mm rocket were Communist.

Or Communist-backed.

So yeah, this squad was definitely part of this so-called Turkish Peoples Liberation Army, wittingly or unwittingly playing puppet while the U.S.S.R. pulled the strings.

And somehow he had to follow the bastards right into their lair.

Bolan had already considered and rejected a headlong pursuit of the escaped commander and his driver. From the chopper recon, Bolan knew that the roads in this area branched and forked and criss-crossed frequently, and often in patterns that hardly seemed to make logical sense. The terrorist leader knew those roads, and it would not have taken him long to obscure his backtrack completely.

Recon, surveillance, and advance intelligence were always the bedrock of the Executioner's assaults. And despite the leader's escape, this firefight had given Bolan a wedge in that direction.

Whatever battlefield instinct had made Bolan spare the single Turkish fighter was about to pay off.

The Turk advanced slowly across the killground. His hands were above his shoulders, but he was not looking at the black-clad man waiting for him. Instead he was staring at the bodies littering the ground around him, the bleeding, still-warm remains of what had been his squad.

He stopped in front of Bolan and looked up at him, then turned and made a sweeping gesture that took in the entire hell's half-acre behind him. He said something in Turkish, and his tone was both awed and resigned.

He was a little dark guy, not more than five-six. Bolan figured him to be in his mid-twenties at the most. His uniform was torn at one knee, his blouse was smeared with dirt, and he had lost his beret. He had straight dark hair cut short, a mustache, and a longish nose that hooked a little at the end and featured a good-sized bump at the bridge, as if it had been broken a couple of times.

"Turn around," Bolan said, his voice low and hard.

The Turk looked at Bolan quizzically. He did not seem particularly afraid, nor did he look very dangerous. But he was one of them, and Bolan had not come this far by taking needless chances.

Bolan lowered the barrel of the M-16 toward the ground and whirled it in a circular motion.

The Turk got it then. He turned his back to Bolan and raised his hands a little higher.

Bolan patted him down quickly but expertly. He was unarmed. In fact, he carried nothing at all in his pockets and no identification of any kind, although Bolan doubted whether he could have read it anyway.

"What's your name?" Bolan said.

The little Turk cocked his head.

"Name," Bolan said again. He jabbed himself in the chest with a finger and said, "Phoenix," then pointed to the Turk and gave him a questioning look.

The Turk tried to say, "Phoenix," but didn't even come close. But he understood what Bolan wanted. He pointed to himself and said something that sounded like "Horuk."

"Let's make it 'Hook,'" Bolan said, mostly to himself. But the Turk caught it and nodded vigorously. Apparently "Hook" was close enough.

The little Turk started to say something else, but Bolan cut him off with a gesture toward the Rover.

Bolan motioned the Turk into the driver's seat, then climbed in on the other side.

Two parallel lines of bare dirt cutting through the grass formed the only direction marker. And they didn't tell Bolan much.

The Turkish terrorists had to be about ready to start shipping the opium. Too many factors were coming up that way. For one, if they were willing to take the chance of firing on an unmarked chopper, not knowing what kind of retaliation it could bring, they were ready to move out.

So the numbers were tight. Once the dope left Turkey and was distributed to the underground labs in France and Italy, it would be one hell of an impossible job to stop it. A drug pipeline was like a rusting battleship—plug one leak, and three more open up.

That pipeline had to be cut off now, at the source.

The trouble lay in finding that damn mine where the terrorists were based.

Sure, Bolan was sitting next to a guy who knew exactly where it was. There were just two problems.

First, neither of them could understand the other. The Turk *could* lead Bolan to the base—could and would. Bolan knew more than a little about getting information out of reluctant subjects. If only they could communicate. Drawings and diagrams might work—or might not. They could just confuse the matter. Besides, there was no way to tell whether the Turk would spill the straight goods. Mack Bolan knew how to tell when an enemy was lying—but not when the guy was talking in a foreign language.

That led to the second problem. Bolan could not forget that Hook was one of the terrorists.

Yet despite the language gap, Bolan did have an intuitive feeling about the little Turk, a feeling he was inclined to accept. When he thought about it, he realized he had little choice anyway. Right now Bolan's combat sense was telling him that there was more to this man than his association with the TPLA indicated. But there was nothing logical about it. Ten minutes earlier, the man had been advancing on Bolan behind a spray of automatic weapons fire.

Yet Bolan was heeding a gut feeling that somehow the little guy did not *belong*.

Bolan said, "Hook."

The Turk turned to him.

Bolan pointed his finger sharply ahead, then shrugged his shoulders in an exaggerated gesture of inquiry.

The Turk pointed in the same direction and nodded once, sharply.

Okay. *If* the little Turk understood what Bolan was asking—and *if* he wasn't pulling a cute double-cross, and there was no logical reason to believe he wasn't—then *maybe*, just maybe, this was the break Bolan had coming.

Yeah, some break. A chance to follow a bunch of Russian-armed Turkish terrorists right into their den.

It was the only break Mack Bolan had.

He settled back in the seat and said, "Tally-ho, Hook."

13

"You must have been out of your mind," Richard Hagen said. "Take my word for it."

He picked the loaf of bread off the floor, where the guard had thrown it, tore it in half, and brought one half to Adamian on the bed. The other man was sitting up straight, and he seemed pretty much recovered from whatever punishment the bastards had dished out to him. Hagen looked at the big Armenian with new-found respect. There was definitely something more here than just a middle-aged businessman. Adamian seemed transformed. There was a fire in his eyes, a hard set to his expression, despite the fix they were in. Then Hagen got it: there was in Adamian a glimmer of that same quality he had seen in the other men, the slim blonde and the man in black.

If only the guy didn't have a belfry full of bats.

"I was naive," Adamian said. He tore off a hunk from his piece of bread and chewed vigorously, wincing only slightly at the tenderness still in his jaw. "Naive and, yes, stupid. But Dikran, my heart was good, even if my head was clouded."

"Richard," Hagen cut in. "Dick to my friends, but no 'Dikran.' And no Hagopian either, if you don't mind. The name is Richard V. Hagen."

He stared critically at his half of the bread. The coarse-grained loaf was speckled with what looked suspiciously like dead insects. Hagen grimaced, then shrugged and took a good bite. He hadn't been fed since the night before.

"Why do you insist on denying your heritage?"

Adamian said quietly. "You were born an Armenian, and you shall die an Armenian. Your denial will not change this."

"I grew up in America," Hagen shot back. "I was raised an American, and I was right-hand man to an American president. You can't get much more American than that, friend." He paused, then continued more quietly. "What's Armenia to me?"

"Don't you remember 1915? That was the year a million of our people were killed. By the Turks."

"I don't *remember* it," Hagen said. "I hadn't been born in 1915, and neither had you."

Adamian finished the last of his share of the bread. He leaned back against the wall and eyed the other man. "Another once said something like that. He said, 'Who still talks nowadays of the extermination of the Armenians?' "

"Yeah?" Hagen said without much interest. "Who?"

"Adolf Hitler," Adamian said. "To Hermann Goering, just before the German invasion of Poland."

Hagen looked up in surprise at the big man across from him. He suddenly felt uncomfortable under his gaze, and he turned away.

"So, Dikran, maybe you do understand, just a little," Adamian said. "Maybe you are right. Maybe I am out of my mind. But if I am obsessed, it is a good and strong obsession. I believed that this thing could be done, that by winning a small victory over the Turks we could draw the attention of the world, make them understand what happened, how our homeland was taken from us. Maybe, if we were very strong and very lucky, we could even gain a portion of it back. I know now that part was a futile dream."

Hagen picked up the green glass bottle of water the guard had left near the door. He sniffed at it cautiously. The bottle smelled as though it had previously held kerosene. Hagen took a cautious pull, then handed the bottle to Adamian, who drank more deeply.

"This man Paradine," Adamian went on. "This man you directed to me told me he could supply me with a fighting force, a force that could make a blow for freedom in our homeland."

"I had no idea . . . " Hagen began.

"I know that, Dikran. You knew nothing of my World Armenian Congress or of my plans, and I have no anger for you."

"How could you believe this guy? What on earth made you trust him?"

"Several things," Adamian said. "First, he was able to get to you. This suggested that he knew his way around certain . . . shall we say, circles. Second, he knew of me, knew of my support of certain groups. He knew details so intimate that he could only have been a . . . a professional himself."

"What groups?"

"A few organizations highly committed to the Armenian cause."

Hagen stared at the other man with a look of growing horror. "I don't believe it," he said slowly. "You were giving money to *terrorists*?"

"I was supporting the movement to restore the Armenian homeland to its people."

"And committing treason at the same time. Do I have to tell you the U.S. stand on terrorism?"

"You don't have to tell me anything," Adamian said evenly. "The Armenians have always been good and loyal citizens of the United States. Did you know that in the first census of the Jamestown Colony in 1620 there is listed a 'Martin the Armenian'?"

Hagen shook his head in exasperation. He had seen some one-track minds in his day, but Adamian took the money. "Look," he said. "This is getting us nowhere. What we've got to figure out first is what the hell we're doing here."

"I don't know."

"They've got your money," Hagen said, half to himself. "Why didn't they just take it and run?" He turned back to Adamian. "Think, man," he urged. "If we've got a chance—and I've got my doubts on that score—this is our only shot."

"I can make some guesses," Adamian said thoughtfully. "I am well known as an Armenian-American, active in various causes of our people. They could use me to embarrass our adopted country, or our cause, or both. You are an Armenian as well, whether you accept the fact or not. You also have vast and powerful contacts, both in the United States, from your former position, and in other parts of the world, from your present one. They will no doubt try to exploit them."

"Then what was the idea of that attack on your home?"

"The idea," Adamian said succinctly, "was to kill me. Someone had learned of my plan, and . . ." His voice trailed off, but his mouth remained open, and a shocked look creased his features.

"Paradine," Hagen said. "He put you in the crossfire, sold you out!"

"Of course," Adamian said, letting his breath out slowly. "Then when the attack was foiled, Paradine had no trouble falling back on his second plan. He convinced me that now was the time for the fight in the homeland." The enormity of it staggered Adamian. "He's a professional, all right. He actually went ahead and set up the contingency plan for my transport here, even though he never expected to use it."

"The double-crossing son of a bitch," Hagen said, awe and rage mixed in his voice. Then something almost like hope came into it. "Speaking of professionals, what about the other one?"

"The man in black?"

"Yeah. Who the hell was he?"

Adamian looked solemnly at the other. "A friend, Dikran. I am sure of that." He turned and looked vaguely at the far wall, as if he were seeing those events of two days and a half-world ago. "I have never seen anything like that man. He fought like a tiger, Dikran, cold and cunning and without anger. But when he spoke to me, he was not an animal but a man. A good man, and true. I know that in my heart."

"Whoever he was, he had to know something about what was going down," Hagen said. "That means...."

"That he may still be following the events of our little...adventure?" Adamian asked. "That he may represent a hope?"

The door of the shack swung open. Two men came in, but although they were in uniform, it was not the uniform of the Turks. These men were garbed in green camouflage fatigues, high black combat boots sporting an immaculate shine, and billed caps pulled low. Both men were big, well over six feet tall, and nearly as broad across the shoulders as the door. Each carried a holstered autopistol on the hip, a bayonet opposite, and an automatic rifle held at parade rest.

Even to an untrained observer like Hagen, it was obvious that these men were different from those outside, and not only in uniform. The erect postures, the spit-and-polish outfits, the well-tended weapons—there was an aura about these hardmen. They were professionals, born to the uniform, the gun, the knife.

The men outside were just terrorists, killers. These men were warriors.

These were men in control.

One of them gestured with the barrel of his rifle. Hagen stepped back and sat down beside Adamian.

Then a third man entered the shack.

This man was tall, almost slim, with longish blond hair. He wore light-colored canvas twill slacks, hiking boots, and a nylon Windbreaker zipped halfway up over a dark-colored T-shirt, not quite high enough to hide the heavy, square butt of his pistol. His eyes were hidden behind wire-rimmed sunglasses with very dark lenses. His skin was tanned, and in age he could have been anywhere between thirty and forty-five.

Paradine.

"Oh, shit," Hagen said.

"You know, Mr. Adamian," Paradine was saying, "it's interesting how well things can work out if one has an open mind. As a shrewd man, I believe you will appreciate that when you hear what I have to say."

Paradine paced slowly to the end of the small shack and turned around to face the two men on the cot. *The bastard's getting a kick out of this*, Hagen thought. The two hardmen flanked the door impassively.

"When you first came to my attention a year ago. . ." Paradine began, but Adamian cut in.

"But you contacted me only two months ago."

"That is correct. But I heard of you long before that. You see, the money you were channeling to the SALA—the so-called Secret Liberation Army of Armenia—found its way there through me. A man in my business has many contacts of that sort."

"Just what is your business?" Hagen said.

"The same as yours, Mr. Hagen. I'm a consultant."

"What you are," Hagen said, "is a murdering son of a bitch who doesn't even care whom he murders for."

Paradine smiled thinly. "Very good, Mr. Hagen. That shows what I believe you call 'spunk.' "

Paradine turned his head slightly and nodded almost imperceptibly. One of the hardmen stepped forward and put his hand on Hagen's neck, just above the shoulder.

An incredible lightning bolt of pain shot down Hagen's arm, and his head felt as if it were about to explode. His eyes bulged in his head, and then everything went black for a moment. Then he could see again, but the pain continued to pulse in his head like something alive.

"So much for spunk," he heard Paradine say. "Please don't interrupt again. Karel has a physician's sensitive touch with pressure points. That particular one, if pressed with a bit more force, results in a neat severing of the jugular vein. And frankly, I'm not quite ready for that yet."

He turned back to Adamian. "However, Mr. Hagen is correct in that I do work for whoever will pay my price. I was quite happy to gather a few of your friends in the SALA together and set you up as their military commander. Whether they would have followed you in your folly is another matter, one in which I had no intention of getting involved."

Hagen dragged himself to his feet and made it to the cot. The pain was down to a dull throbbing.

"We expected the possibility of opposition to the attack on your house," Paradine went on. "One of my own men handled the preliminary reconnaissance."

For the first time some emotion came into Paradine's voice. "His name was Ramor, and he was killed, gentlemen." Paradine's lips were set in a thin line. "He was a good man, and he was killed by your friend in black."

He spun on them suddenly, and involuntarily Hagen pulled back. "No doubt you have some fantasy about this man coming to save you," he snapped. "I hope you are right." His voice was low and deadly. "I owe Ramor that man's head. And I mean to have it."

Paradine pulled himself erect and made a visible effort to calm himself. "I am working here for a lucrative client," he went on in a more rational voice. "I don't mind telling you that client is the KGB, because I don't expect that you will be able to exploit that knowledge. You see, I've decided to throw you, Mr. Adamian, as well as you, Mr. Hagen, to the wolves."

The blond man turned to the window and peered reflectively through the dirty glass. "For several years we have been paying local farmers to grow opium poppies—call it an agricultural assistance program, if you like. This country is sixty-eight percent agricultural to begin with, and abysmally poor, especially in the rural areas, so most of the farmers were quite happy to work with us. Those who were not were...dealt with. In those two long buildings across this compound, those poppies are being processed into raw opium. A great deal has already been stockpiled in that abandoned mine shaft."

Paradine turned back to the two men. "Enough to make a lot of drug addicts and prospective drug addicts in your country very happy. The money gained, even after costs, will be enough to equip a small army, and that's just what it will be used for.

"Within a few days, the opium will move out over a prearranged route. It will be delivered to a prearranged consortium of buyers, who will refine it into heroin and feed it into their own well-established distribution lines.

"In the meantime, small arms, explosives, and light artillery will be delivered to various cadres of the Turkish Peoples' Liberation Army around the country. The bulk of the TPLA's strength is massed near the capital of Ankara. Within hours, our TPLA friends will have seized the government, which is currently leaning toward the West. My friends in the U.S.S.R. feel confident that the new Turkish government will be quite willing to, shall we say, make friends."

Paradine clasped his hands together in a gesture of completion. "You see how neatly it dovetails. The

Soviet Union benefits by gaining Turkey as a strategic and undivided ally, its first toehold on the Mediterranean. They are also quite happy to see this flood of heroin enter your country, and the social chaos it will most certainly cause. My little TPLA puppets gain the government. And I receive a generous commission for my efforts on my client's behalf."

"And we serve as the insurance policy," Hagen said.

"Correct," Paradine said. "I am almost indebted to your little guardian angel in black. The death of six Turkish fanatics and two Italian gangsters is, now that I reflect on it, quite worth having you still alive." Then his face hardened again. He spun on his heel and spoke directly to the men flanking the door. "But not Ramor," he said, biting off the words. "He was a man, not a mindless sheep. His life will be avenged. With a life," he vowed.

"Your country is going to be very embarrassed," Paradine went on grimly. "And you, gentlemen, are going to be very dead. You are going to play the parts of the two Armenian activists, so desperate for the promise of an Armenian homeland that you are willing to connive in this terrorist revolution. Not only will your government come under severe criticism—especially since you, Mr. Hagen, are a former top official in that government—but it should keep the fire of Turkish-Armenian conflict burning for a long time."

Paradine laughed hollowly. "But don't worry. Your deaths will not go. . . ."

Whatever Paradine was about to say was lost in a sudden commotion outside. Paradine started for the window to see what it was about, but the door suddenly burst open. Hagen recognized the man he had seen ordering around the other terrorist troops. His uniform was torn and dirty, and his red beret was gone. His aide was cowering behind him.

Everything of the conversational manner Paradine

had adopted was gone. In its place was that jarring aura of something hard and vicious that Hagen had noticed on first meeting the man.

Suddenly, the guy radiated barely contained violence, like a grenade with a missing pin.

"How dare you burst in like this, Takim?" Paradine demanded, his voice filled with menace.

The terrorist leader spewed out a torrent of excited Turkish. Paradine snapped a command in the same tongue, and Takim faltered and then was quiet.

Paradine's two hardmen grabbed Takim and hustled him out of the shack. Paradine followed, without even looking at his two prisoners again.

Hagen went to the window and peered out. A Rover was parked near the center of the compound. Takim's aide was standing next to the driver's side, a sickly look on his face. Takim himself was looking up at Paradine and talking so loudly that Hagen could hear the faint sounds inside the shack.

Takim pointed a finger at Paradine's chest, and Paradine slapped it away. Takim started to move toward him, then looked at the two hardmen flanking the blond mercenary and seemed to change his mind. He stood there watching as Paradine and the hardmen turned and left him standing there.

Takim spun on his heel, took two steps, and slammed his fist into his driver's face.

The driver's nose shattered in a spray of blood. He slammed back against the Rover, then slumped slowly to the ground, the thick, dark redness bubbling out of the middle of his face. Takim stood above him, glowering at the only outlet for his rage he could find.

"Dikran," Adamian said behind him.

"Yeah," Hagen said, not bothering to correct the name Adamian used.

"He's here. In Turkey."

Hagen turned. "Who's here?"

"The man who saved my life. The big man in black."

"My God," Hagen breathed. "How...?"

"The Turk leader, the one Paradine called Takim. He said his convoy was attacked. All his men were killed except the driver. He said it was one man. Then Paradine cut him off."

"One man. How the hell could one man take on a whole terrorist squad? I saw those boys leave here. There were about twenty of them, and they had a rocket launcher and a machine gun and automatic rifles. A one-man attack would be suicide."

"You did not see what he did the other night in Beverly Hills. This is no ordinary man. He fights like an army."

"How do you know that the one Takim saw is him?"

"I don't. But we must have hope, and we must be ready. We must not give up." Adamian drew himself erect, and the light seemed to come back into his eyes. "It is not only for the sake of our lives. We must do what is right."

Hagen stared at the other man.

"All my life I have blindly hated the Turks," Adamian said. "But it has taken these people to show me what blind hatred truly is. These people feed on hate, are nurtured by it like mother's milk. They are also Turks, yes, but what they really are is reptiles, the worms of the earth. They are willing to sacrifice brother and stranger alike for their ends."

Adamian seemed to take strength from the power of his own words. "You and I, Dikran, we cannot let them make us a part of this. Yes, I was wrong, and I understand that finally. Wrong to feed on my own blind hatred of an entire people, wrong to involve you in that hatred."

"Fine," Hagen said cynically. "So what do we do?"

"We prepare. There will come the time when we

will have to act. This man in black is strong, incredibly strong. But how can even he expect to storm this entire compound single-handedly? We must be prepared to help, to seize the moment and act like men."

"*If* it's him," Hagen said. "*If* there ever is a moment."

"Trust me, Dikran."

Richard Hagen suddenly realized with a crystal clarity that he was facing death. Yet the realization brought not the cold chill of unutterable fear, but the calmness and serenity that now, at this time, like no other in his life, he could take complete responsibility for his actions.

And Adamian was right. They would have to be the actions of a man.

He offered his hand, and Adamian took it.

"You and me, Marko," Hagen said. "And God help us both."

14

Mack Bolan did not consider himself a complex man. When describing him, all who knew the man well spoke of his quiet compassion and innate intelligence. It was also true that this man who had come to be known as the Executioner understood the responsibilities that came with his adopted life as a warrior, and he tried to live accordingly. In his long campaign against the Mafia, Mack Bolan had never launched a strike unless he had absolute and positive identification of its target. His first rule was to take the greatest possible precautions to insure that no noncombatants would be caught in the crossfire. Even on the occasions when he was forced to react instinctively to ambush or counterstrike, his almost extrasensory combat instincts guided him to avoid involving the innocent or engaging the officers of any law enforcement agency, often at the risk of his own life.

Add to that the fact that the guy was also a self-taught psychologist, a natural offshoot of his lifelong interest in observing and responding to his fellow beings. Over the course of his thirty-eight Mafia campaigns, Bolan had come to know the enemy better than the enemy knew itself.

Using this knowledge, he perfected role camouflage to a high art. He did not use a disguise per se; instead, he assumed a character with such confidence and force of will that the enemy was unable to perceive him as anyone except who he claimed to be. He became able to infiltrate the inner Mob sanctums almost at will. Finally, Bolan actually established himself as a highly respected (and equally feared) Mafia enforcer, in the identity of the near-mythical Omega, the Black Ace whose power rivaled that of the *capi* themselves.

Mack Bolan had also engaged in a thoughtful, and ongoing, program of self-analysis, to insure that he himself understood and was at peace with the way of life he had chosen. His commitment to awareness of self and of the world in which he existed was complete. The numerous entries in the journals he had kept since the age of fourteen, some of which amounted to sophisticated philosophical essays in their own right, bore ample witness to the man's quest for knowledge and correct perception.

Intelligent, quick-witted, adaptable, alert to himself. Sure, the guy was all of that. A tendency toward introspection, maybe.

But no, Mack Bolan did not consider himself a complex man.

Despite the stubbornness with which he would seek answers to the questions he believed important, the man did not overintellectualize. After all, the idea was to clarify, not to obscure.

It was this simple: a lot of people liked to say there was no such thing as black or white. Mack Bolan knew those people were wrong.

There were times, many times, when good and evil stood in clear and stark opposition. And the only way any honest and moral person could avoid *that* truth was to turn his back.

It was the British statesman Edmund Burke who wrote in 1795, "The only thing necessary for the triumph of evil is for good men to do nothing."

Mack Bolan was constitutionally unable to "do nothing." In fact, he could not remember a time when he had not instinctively understood that it is the duty of Moral Man to preserve good and eliminate evil, actively, wherever either is found.

The rediscovery of that simple opposition between

black and white was what first triggered the Executioner's one-man war. Three members of his family, honest, working-class people in the eastern city of Pittsfield, were dead, another seriously wounded, all victims of the vicious, greedy, amoral hand of the Mafia, the omnipresent crime cartel that some misguided people insisted did not even exist.

It existed, all right. And it was so powerful that its greasy mitts touched the lives of every single American, whether or not they felt it. So great was the power of *La Cosa Nostra*—This Thing of Ours, the Mob smugly called itself—that it constituted a virtual second government of the United States, an invisible empire that the legally vested authorities had found impossible to touch in anything but the most impotent of ways. And they had been trying for over fifty years.

Income tax evasion or unfair trade practices. Those were about the only charges the law enforcement boys had been able to make stick. And the Mafiosi would pay their fines, laugh in the judges' faces, and go right back to their regular pursuits.

Those pursuits didn't have a hell of a lot to do with taxes or trade.

They had to do with extortion, coercion, and intimidation of honest citizens. Not to mention drug peddling, crooked gambling, the enslavement of young women to a life of prostitution—and murder.

Oh yeah. Murder was the favorite expedient of those boys in the expensive, tailored suits.

So okay, there it was, in simple black and white. And anyone who couldn't see which were the good guys and which were the bad could go stick his head back in the sand, where it had apparently been for so long.

"I am not their judge," Bolan wrote in his journal during the Mafia campaigns. "I am not their jury. They have condemned themselves through their actions, through the lives they have chosen, with free will and foreknowledge. They themselves have rendered the verdict: guilty as charged.

"And I am their Executioner."

Bolan took that perception the length and breadth of America, eliminating that clear and present evil wherever it had taken root. Despite what the Mafia had done to his family, his motive was not vengeance. He was simply taking care of a job that had been botched for too long.

At first there was public outrage. This was vigilante justice; this was not the American way. Then people started opening their eyes and looking around. The country was getting well again, and it was damn sure that no one was suffering from the absence of several hundred of these bums who for years had made American society their personal pea patch. The carping mouths suddenly clamped shut.

There was something to be said for radical surgery when the patient came out of it whole and alive.

When the Mafia glutton had been brought to its knees, and then to its belly, Mack Bolan finally felt able to put that campaign behind him. Yet he knew perfectly well that he had won only a battle. The war itself would never be won until Animal Man, whatever his race, nationality, politics, or criminal ambition, was eradicated from the face of the earth.

That was why, on a rainy Saturday afternoon in New York's Central Park, Mack Bolan became no more and Colonel John Macklin Phoenix rose from his ashes. The echoes of Bolan's last campaign against the Mafia were still reverberating when a violent explosion turned the Executioner's Warwagon into a gutted hulk of twisted scrap-metal. As far as the world knew and believed, Mack Bolan died in that explosion.

In fact, the only occupant of Bolan's mobile base and battle-fortress-on-wheels was one Marco Minotti. In the wake of Bolan's final Big Apple Blitz, Crazy Marco, the Mafia hardman, descended from snarling depravity into babbling lunacy, a pathetic imitation of a human being. His death was a mercy killing.

The newly minted Colonel Phoenix had himself pressed the remote button that triggered the autodestruct system, supposedly obliterating Mack Bolan. It was his own ironic way of reaffirming his commitment to walk yet another mile of the warrior's path.

In accepting the call of the President of the United States, the Executioner knew that he was making trade-offs. He no longer had to fight alone, and he would no longer have the absolute freedom of action and reaction he had grown used to. Not only that, but in exchange for the large degree of autonomy he would retain, he would be taking on far greater responsibility. Any failure on his part would now almost certainly have direct and immediate results.

At best, a Bolan misstep could embarrass the United States.

At worst, it could threaten the safety of the entire free world, up to and including nuclear holocaust.

So yeah, the stakes had just gone up. But the game hadn't changed, and it was one that Mack Bolan knew how to play better than any man on the face of the globe.

Bolan had never been especially interested in politics, and during the Mafia campaigns he had little time to keep up on current world events. What he had learned in the time since, as the Stony People were being organized and the Stony Man Farm base fitted out, had opened the man's eyes. The threat of world terrorism was real, extensive, and immediate.

The old black and white once again. Most of these vermin, who liked to give themselves noble-sounding titles like "freedom fighters" or "liberation front" or "people's revolutionaries," owed their allegiance to domination, power, and financial gain. Maybe some of them did honestly subscribe to higher ideals, but the violence they randomly employed in the name of these ideals, violence that often killed innocent people, made them just as bad as the others. Taken as a whole, the international terrorist community represented the greatest evil Mack Bolan had ever faced, and they were more in need of his "surgical" talents than even the Mafia had been.

This self-styled Turkish Peoples' Liberation Army, for example—it was no more representative of the Turkish nation than Turkish baths or Turkish towels. No doubt, given the chance, they'd loudly proclaim that their revolution was for the good of the "people." They just happened to conveniently forget the tens of thousands, maybe even millions, of other "people" they were quite willing to enslave and degrade with the horrors of heroin addiction.

Then there was the man who called himself Paradine. His kind were the worst—the bloodsuckers, the leeches sucking at the cancerous tissue of worldwide violence. The mercenaries, the ones who were willing to do anything for anybody if the price was right. These were the cool, calculated killers who didn't even bother to profess sympathy with any cause.

Their cause was terror. Their purpose was to promote death and destruction wherever and whenever possible, because it was this on which they fed, like vultures picking through rotting carrion.

Sure, it got complex in its parts. In Beverly Hills Turkish terrorists led by a washed-up Mafioso try to assassinate a dozen influential Armenian-Americans. In Paris, Armenian hit men take out a Turkish diplomat. Terrorism begets terrorism, and the longer it is allowed to go on unchecked, the more people like Paradine are allowed to profit from it—and the more it blooms and thrives and multiplies.

While the real "people," the people who matter, are forced to cower in fear.

Fear. Intimidation. Terror. Complex emotions, tangled conflicts, but simple, direct, and horrible results.

So you fight it, using means just as simple and

direct. That was Mack Bolan's reluctant realization.

If killing and destruction were the only languages they understood, that was what you spoke to them.

In short, simple, deadly sentences.

So it was a different game than before, sure. Not only higher stakes, but a higher payoff, win or lose.

Mack Bolan had no intention of losing.

At the bottom line, that was just how simple it would have to be.

The little Turk whom Bolan had dubbed Hook interrupted his thoughts with an incomprehensible torrent of Turkish accompanied by a vigorous gesture to the right of the trail they were following. But Bolan had already spotted what Hook found so exciting. Even during his contemplation of his duties in this place and time, a part of his mind stayed on combat alert, sharp-tuned to the external, scanning the surrounding hills for anything that didn't belong, checking the backtrack for unwanted company.

Hook pulled the Rover to a stop and continued to point. Here the rugged road followed a fair-sized creek through a shallow valley with gently sloping grassy hills on either side. The hill to the right was bisected by a smaller stream that flowed into the one on the valley floor, and about halfway up the slope, about 200 meters from where Bolan sat, there was a stand of cypress trees. Nearby there was a stone hut that looked as if it had been there for quite a while.

Two women stood near the stone hut and stared curiously down at them. Both were swathed in shapeless blouses and dull-colored skirts that hung to the ground, and they wore kerchiefs over their hair. The kerchiefs covered their chins and mouths as well, so that Bolan could get only an indistinct impression of the women's eyes, as if they were wearing masks in reverse. Even their hands were hidden somewhere in the voluminous folds of their clothing.

A third woman was walking toward Bolan. She

had already started down the hill when they stopped, and now she was less than fifty meters away. She was dressed the same as the other women on the hill, but she did things for the coarse clothing that the other two could not. She was in her mid-twenties, and the loose white blouse could not hide her high, full breasts, nor could the drape of the skirt conceal the flare of her hips. She wore no kerchief, and her jet-black hair fell straight to her shoulders, framing an open, olive face with a full red mouth and dark eyes that seemed to flash.

She was carrying an AK-47, and it was trained on Bolan.

Hook shifted into gear and started to rev the motor. Bolan reached over and flicked off the ignition switch.

Hook started to say something, but Bolan cut him off with a raised hand. He stepped cautiously from the Rover, moving slowly and keeping his hands away from his own weapons.

The girl stopped a few paces from him. The rifle was steady in her hands. She looked Bolan over calmly, her gaze sweeping him from head to toe, taking in the black skinsuit bedecked with armament, the handguns at his hip and shoulder, and the Ingram, slung from the strap at his neck.

"I'm not going to harm you," Bolan said to the girl. He knew she wouldn't understand the words, but he hoped she would catch something from his tone.

Her eyes widened slightly. She leveled the rifle directly on his middle.

For just a moment, Bolan wondered if he had made a mistake. He was not about to fire on a woman, not without knowing who she was and what she represented. Besides, there was something about her—some assurance that seemed to go far beyond her years—that told him she was not his enemy. But if he were wrong, just about five pounds of pressure on the trigger of the Kalashnikov would splatter his guts all over the Turkish landscape. At ten paces, the girl wasn't about to miss.

"I know how to use this," the girl said. "If anyone should be worried about being harmed, it's you." Her English was nearly accentless, but there was an offbeat lilt to its rhythm.

Bolan kept his expression calm and his eyes on the girl, but his mind was racing. She spoke English! That meant she could translate for him, and he could interrogate Hook. And that meant he could find out the location of the terrorist base.

And what was probably the biggest raw opium stash in the world.

The numbers were running down; Bolan knew that and it was gnawing at him. The terrorist commander would be back at the base by now, and they wouldn't be holding back any longer. They'd know the opium would have to move, and soon.

Once it did, no man could stop it.

"Keep your hands above your head," the girl said, gesturing up with the rifle barrel. "Who are you?" she asked, when Bolan had complied.

"A friend." This girl was too valuable. He had to have her help, whether she was willing to give it freely or not. Too damn much was at stake. She was standing close enough. Drop to a half-crouch, roll and come up under the gun, jam a finger behind the trigger if possible, twist and wrench to break her grip. Bolan rehearsed the movement in his mind, then tensed, ready to use it.

"There was another who spoke English," the girl said. "He was not a friend." She nodded toward Hook without taking her eyes from Bolan. "What are you doing with him?"

As long as she was asking questions, she wasn't going to shoot. And she would probably be hurt if he jumped her—there was no gentle way to disarm someone holding a fully automatic spraygun. But damn, the numbers were falling.

The girl snapped out something in Turkish. From her tone it sounded like a question.

Hook answered with a rush of words that she finally had to cut off.

"He says you fought against him," the girl said. "He says you killed all his comrades."

Hook interjected another burst of Turkish.

"He says you saved his life."

"I could have killed him," Bolan said levelly. "I didn't."

"For him it's the same." She lowered the rifle slightly and furrowed her brow in thought. The effect was quite pretty. "He's Muslim. He should have died with his brothers. When you let him live at first, he should have killed you or died trying." She smiled without humor, showing a row of perfect white teeth, made whiter by contrast to her olive skin. "He decided he'd rather live, but of course that means he will be killed as a traitor and a coward if he goes back. He says he will be your comrade instead, and he pledges absolute faith to you in word and deed, as long as he lives."

Bolan glanced over his shoulder. The little Turk nodded and grinned. But there was only one thing Bolan wanted from him: the detailed directions to the terrorist stronghold.

"Is everything I've heard the truth?" the girl asked.

"Yes."

She gazed at him, then took her eyes from him for the first time to look over her shoulder. Bolan made no move toward her. The two other women were still standing near the hut, staring down at them as though this was a play being performed for their benefit, one that they did not appreciate. The girl nibbled at her lip in thought.

Then she lowered the rifle.

"You're here to stop them, aren't you," the girl

said. It was a statement, not a question. "Don't lie to me. I'll know if you do."

"I'm here to stop them," Bolan said. "And I don't have much time."

"Come up to the hut. There is food. You must question the little Turk, and I'll translate. I can help in other ways, too."

Bolan allowed himself a grin. Whoever she was, whatever she was doing talking perfect colloquial English in the middle of the Turkish wilderness while protecting her home with a Russian-made weapon, he knew one thing: this was one hell of a woman.

He reached back into the Rover and retrieved the '203 and said to Hook, "Let's go," gesturing with his head.

All the way up the hill, Hook jabbered excitedly. Bolan let the incomprehensible words wash over him. His eyes were on the sensuously swaying hips of the girl as she trudged up the hill in front of him, but even that attractive picture was not really registering in his mind.

Bolan's mind was on a vision of another hill; a hill of white powder, as big as a haystack.

Dream dust, they called it. Snow. Poppy power.

Bolan called it living death, injected into the veins of society.

He shook the image out of his head.

With the help of this extraordinary woman, Mack Bolan was going to inject a little medicine of his own. Where it would do the most good.

15

"There is only one thing worse than a fool," Paradine said in Turkish. "That is a coward. And you, Colonel Takim, are both."

Takim let out a guttural snarl and reached for the autopistol at his belt.

The hardman named Karel stepped past Paradine and slammed the barrel of his rifle against the side of Takim's head. The Turk's red beret flew off in one direction, and his pistol clattered across the hard-rock floor of the mine shaft. He sat down hard and shook his head groggily. The two hardmen stood above him, their AK-47s trained on him.

"Don't ever try to draw a weapon on me, Takim," Paradine said. "These men are trained to protect my life at all times and at all costs." Paradine held up his thumb and forefinger, an inch apart. "This is how far you were from death." He closed the two fingers and snapped them, and Takim started involuntarily. "Now," Paradine said in a lighter voice. "Let's try to work together, like the allies we are supposed to be."

Paradine nodded, and the two hardmen stepped back. Takim pulled himself to his feet. It cost him some effort and some pain, but he could not let this man talk down to him. Takim wiped at the side of his head, where the rifle barrel had struck him. His fingertips came away smeared with blood.

"I did not know. . ." he began calmly.

"You didn't know!" Paradine exploded. He stared at Takim, his eyes hidden behind the dark glasses but the malevolence radiating palpably from them.

This man was dangerous. Takim had not manipulated his way to where he was now without learning something about people. He knew that this Paradine had allegiance only to himself, and he was coming to understand that the man was a monomaniac as well. Paradine was obsessed with a single idea: the successful completion of the assignment for which he had been commissioned. Takim knew he had no commitment to a cause; his entire reason for being was to satisfy his own ego by proving his power and dominance. A dangerous man indeed. One who would let nothing stand in his way.

Especially not one black-clad infidel.

"You don't know how to fight, you stupid sheep!" Paradine ranted on. "You are going to lead the revolutionary overthrow of an entire government. But first you must learn how to overcome one man."

Paradine's voice was thick with sarcasm. "A platoon of twenty-five men, trained in the fighting skills, dedicated to the cause. And what is the outcome? Twenty-three of them are dead, a busload of valuable armament is destroyed, and the brave commander, the terrible Colonel Takim, flees like an aged woman clutching her skirts around her legs."

Takim drew himself erect and stared steadily at the other man. The two hardmen stared at him from behind the stoic masks that were their faces. Takim did not let his own expression reveal his discomfort. It was bad enough that he had to take orders from the blond infidel. He would not take his abuse as well.

"Yes," Takim said, his voice reasonably steady. "It was one man. But I tried to tell you in the shack. This was a man like no other I have ever seen, dressed all in black like a dervish, and a face like the granite of the walls of this mine, walking through the fire like an avenging demon."

Paradine stiffened, and again the eyes behind the dark glasses seemed to bore into Takim.

"A tall man," Paradine said, half to himself. "Dark, very hard around the mouth, broad in the shoulders. A fighting man."

"Yes," Takim said. "Then you know him."

"I know who he is, yes," Paradine said quietly. "He is the end of all we have built here, the end of the opium and of the money, and the end of any hope you've ever had of gaining Ankara. Unless he is stopped."

Paradine turned and went a few paces deeper into the mine, then spun on his heel. His face was pallid, wolfish in the harsh yellow glare of the bare bulbs that were strung along the ceiling of the abandoned mine shaft. The light reflected off the dark glasses, and it crossed Takim's mind, not for the first time, that the man looked much like some sort of poisonous insect.

Behind Paradine, crates were piled to the ceiling along both sides of the man-made cave. The sticky-sweet odor of raw, unprocessed opium hung in the fetid air.

"We must begin to ship out tonight," Paradine snapped suddenly. "I will make the necessary arrangements over the radio."

"But the contacts," Takim protested. "All is not yet in readiness."

"I will worry about that," Paradine said. "Your concern is this man in black who seems to be too much for twenty-five Turkish fighting men to handle."

"But. . . ."

"You listen to me, Takim. Two days ago, a man named Ramor died. A *man*, Takim, a soldier and a warrior, not some half-trained gunman like those outside that you call your troops. This man in black killed him." Paradine's voice dropped lower, like a death rattle coming from deep in his throat. "You bring me this man's head, Takim. I speak literally. You bring me this pig's head in a sack."

Takim stared at the blond man. He had known men to become passionately devoted to a cause, but never had he seen bloodlust like this.

"You are to take a dozen men," Paradine said. "You find this black-clad dervish of yours, and you make absolutely sure that he never again interferes with our business here."

"A dozen men," Takim said. "But...."

"Our forces are already depleted below the optimum troop strength that this operation calls for," Paradine said. "And we have no time to call up reinforcements. We must—we *will* succeed on our own." He considered for a moment. "Karel will go with you," he went on. "That makes fourteen against one. Hopefully, your brave fighting Turks will find that a sufficient advantage."

Paradine reached inside his Windbreaker and took out a 9mm Luger. Very deliberately, he worked a cartridge into the chamber. Takim watched. Apprehension, anticipation, and fascination were mixed in his expressions, as if he were watching a man with a flute charm a cobra at a street bazaar.

Paradine simply held the gun at his side. The effect on Takim would have been no more electric had the blond man laid the gun barrel against Takim's temple.

"If you do not kill this man in black this time, Takim, you had better make sure that he kills you."

The hand holding the gun began to tremble. Takim forced himself to look the blond man in the eyes, fought to keep his body erect and still.

"Because if he does not," Paradine said, "I will surely kill you myself."

16

Her name was Kabrina, and yeah, she was something special, all right.

She had been born in this country, she told Mack Bolan, twenty-three years before. Her parents were Kurds, nomads who tended their herds of goats and sheep, sometimes cattle, in the rugged, sparsely populated high country of eastern Turkey. It had been their business for generations. In fact, Kabrina's family traced its lineage back, through oral tradition, to tribes who had roamed this same country a millenium before.

The two other women were her mother and grandmother. Bolan would have had trouble guessing which one was older. Both had lined skin the texture and color of saddle leather, what he could see of it. The menfolk—Kabrina's father and his two brothers—were scouting for summer pasture in the higher country and would not be back for several days.

"I am the only child," Kabrina said. The two older women sat on a bench against the wall, observing Bolan through dark, impassive eyes. "After me my mother could no longer bear offspring. My father was very upset, because no male heir meant the end of the family line. He became angry, then violent. Such resentment is not unknown among the Kurds." She paused and stared at Bolan. "You must not think harshly of him. It is just our way. Besides, it all turned out for the best."

Afraid for her safety, Kabrina's mother sent her to live with an aunt who had married a Turk and settled in Istanbul. An apt pupil in the city school, Kabrina was urged by some European friends to apply for college. She did, and was accepted by a school in Boston.

At the end of four years in America, she graduated with high honors, then returned to Istanbul. It was always her intention to return to her homeland.

"But Istanbul is not my homeland," she told Bolan, "no more than Boston was. I had to go back to my people. I didn't care if my father hated me. People told me I was 'turning my back on civilization,' but they didn't understand. If I were ever to understand how I became who I am, I had to come back." She smiled affectionately at the two older women. "I made my decision even before I heard about the trouble."

"What trouble?" Bolan asked.

"The Kurds are clannish and close-knit," Kabrina answered obliquely. "News travels among them quickly, accurately, and with secrecy, even the length of the country, from here to Istanbul. I learned through this grapevine that my family was being threatened by Turkish soldiers. That is, these men wore the uniform, but they were not of the national forces."

"How did you know that?"

"Because they were asking the people to grow opium for them."

Kabrina paused and looked earnestly at this strange and silent man sitting across from her at the low table in the hut. She had known him for only a few minutes, yet she felt not only that he accepted her, but that he understood her as well. She did not even know his name, but woman's intuition that knew no racial or national boundary told her that what drove him to this place was a lot like what had driven her.

"Opium growing is illegal," Bolan said.

"Yes. But that is not why my family refuses to participate, despite the fact that the Turks offer three times what we, or any Kurd, can make farming or tending a flock. My father simply believes that some things are not right, and that this is one of those things. Most of the other nomads in the area were glad to accept the Turks' offer."

"Your father must be a special kind of man," Bolan said.

"My father is nearly sixty," Kabrina responded. "His two brothers are older. There had been threats—this is what I heard in Istanbul. I was afraid for them, and I came back to help."

"And to fight."

She nodded. "The Turks did not want to accept no for an answer. They came, four of them. They started to push my father around, and he was too old to fight back. Their leader was standing to one side, watching and laughing. I hit him over the head with a shepherd's crook and took his rifle." Bolan followed her glance to the Kalashnikov, which was propped against the wall. "I fired in the air, and they ran like a herd of frightened deer. That was the last we saw of them, but I live in dread that they will return."

"You're a brave woman."

"No," Kabrina said. "It was what I had to do." She smiled ruefully. "My father hated me even more for it. Not only did he still resent my birth as a woman, but now he was embarrassed that I had fought for him. Mother and grandmother treated me like someone who died. The action with the Turks only proved what they suspected all along, that I had been hopelessly corrupted by the infidel Western ways. It was difficult at first."

"Most things worth doing are difficult," Bolan said quietly.

The girl nodded, grateful for the understanding. "For a long time I thought I wouldn't be able to do it. But I had no choice. The Turks are still in the area, and I had to stay to make sure my family was safe. I'm not sure how long I'll remain here when it's over. It won't be for the rest of my life, I understand that. This is what I was, and what I'll always be in some ways, but I'll still grow and develop in other ways too. It's finally beginning to make sense to me."

She watched as Bolan washed down a mouthful of coarse bread with a swig from the bottle of spring water.

"The family accepts me finally," she said, "just as I accept them. And all of us have learned from it."

"You have lived large and well," Bolan told this dark beauty.

She nodded. "I think I have."

Hook was on his knees on the bench at the table, peering over a map of the region that Kabrina produced from a crude pack leaning against the wall. He was frowning in perplexity. He ran a finger along a river, then found the point he was looking for and stabbed at it with one finger and said something to Kabrina.

"He can't be sure," Kabrina translated. "He's never seen a map of the area before, but he thinks he can make a pretty good guess at the location, based on the trips he's made off the base. He thinks it's around here, above the Kara River, east of Erzincan. There are some high mountains there, and the area was the site of a lot of mining development in the past."

"This is important, Kabrina," Bolan said. "I don't have to tell you that. What those people up there are planning is going to hurt all of us, your people and mine. And I don't have much time to stop them."

There was a brief exchange in Turkish.

"He is nearly positive of the location," Kabrina reported. "Anyway, he is certain of the general area, and he says he will be able to lead you to the mine once you reach the vicinity."

Bolan wasn't planning on involving the little Turk in this war. Hook's fight was over. But there was no time to get into that now.

Bolan took paper and pencil from a pocket of the blacksuit and handed them to Hook. "Have him draw a diagram of the camp," he told Kabrina.

Hook wet the tip of the pencil on his tongue, then began to sketch with short, rapid strokes. When he was done, he handed the paper to Bolan and grinned. Through Kabrina, Bolan had him add the features of the surrounding terrain, as well as the access road. With mountains on three sides, the only way in was through the front gate. Okay. Bolan could see a way to make that work for him. He asked a few quick questions about the layout, sketched in the answers, then folded the map and tucked it away in a handy pocket.

"Now ask him about the opium," he directed.

There was no mistaking the surprise on Hook's face. He nodded vigorously and snapped out an answer.

"There is a great deal of it, many crates," Kabrina translated. "Sometimes they had to stack or restack it. They were not told what it was, but he could tell by the smell. Once he and two of his friends stole some and tried to smoke it, but it just made them sick."

"Not as sick as it's going to make a couple of hundred thousand other people if it ever gets out of there," Bolan said grimly. "Okay. Was there ever anyone else in camp besides the TPLA people? Anyone who wasn't Turkish?"

Kabrina spoke rapidly in Turkish, then listened for a moment to the response. "There were other men who came to the camp, but only to visit. A month ago they came to stay. Three of them."

"What did they look like?"

Again the brief exchange. Then, "The one who was the leader was blond, and Hook says he always wears dark glasses, even inside the mine and at night. The other two are very big, tough men, and they are always with him. Everyone is afraid of these men."

Paradine. The man who kept popping up in the middle of all of this. And two hardboys flanking him. Yeah, that fit. That fit just right.

"Anyone else?"

Hook shook his head, but then he started chattering again. Kabrina looked confused. She asked a question. Hook nodded and repeated part of what he had said.

"Two other men were brought into the camp," Kabrina said slowly. "Just before he went out with the convoy. He says they were Armenians."

"Armenians?" Bolan echoed. "Could they have been Americans?"

Hook shrugged in response to the translated question. These two men did not seem to interest him.

"He didn't hear them speak," Kabrina said. "They looked like Armenians to him. He doesn't like Armenians. He doesn't know why, of course. It's just part of most Turks' upbringing."

So okay, there it was. The terrorist nest that Bolan was searching for. Now all he had to do was get there, get in, and blow a couple of tons of opium skyhigh.

Except for the new joker in a deck already crowded with jokers. It looked as if Marko Adamian and Richard Hagen had also found the TPLA camp.

Or it had found them.

"Tell him thanks," Bolan said to the girl. Hook beamed. He started talking in Turkish, haltingly at first, then more rapidly, all the while looking at Bolan. The big man in black lit a cigarette and listened patiently. Finally, the little Turk ran down.

"He wants you to understand that he was one of them, yes," Kabrina said. "But he was never of them. He grew up in the *gecekondu* outside Istanbul, the illegal shantytowns that the poor people throw up at night and the government soldiers tear down in the daytime. His parents died when he was young. He had no job, no education, no home, and no family. The offer of one free hot meal a day was enough to recruit him into the Communist Party."

"When you're hungry, any ideology looks good," Bolan said. "That's one of the ways they prey on the weak."

"Yes," Kabrina said. "And then exploit them for their own gains."

Bolan tamped out his cigarette. It was the same old story. The strong using the others, perverting hunger and poverty and human degradation to their own sordid purposes. Sure, the Communist line was fine if you didn't look too closely. A chicken in every pot, and pie for dessert. It was wonderful, until the bill came.

And it was always more than you could afford.

Offer the carrot, but hide the stick. Then, when you bring the stick out, make it a big one, and hold it over their heads for the rest of their lives.

"After that, he was technically an outlaw, since the CP is illegal," Kabrina said. "He literally had no place else to go, no way out. Many of his comrades were in the same boat. If they complained or disobeyed an order, they were beaten. If they tried to escape, they were executed. They received rudimentary training in military tactics and weaponry, as well as propaganda indoctrination. The idea was to keep them thoroughly immersed in the terrorist cause."

Yeah, some cause. One so despicable that even the conscripts had to be terrorized into fighting. Fighting a war of despair.

These people who had beaten Hook and those like him into submission were human beings in name only. By instinct, motivation, and sheer disregard for the essential humanity of other beings, they were lower than the lowest animals.

Hook added something. Kabrina said, "He wants you to know that he is glad he is no longer forced to be with these evil men. He says you are his savior, and that he is truly your comrade."

Bolan reached across the table and clasped the little Turk's hand. Hook nodded solemnly. This communication needed no translation. It was in the universal language of good men everywhere.

Bolan field-stripped the M-16/203, carefully and quickly cleaned the parts, and reassembled the weapon with sure hands. He did the same with the Ingram, checking the magazines of both guns, then checked and reloaded the Beretta Belle and his AutoMag.

He dug the map out of his pocket and looked it over again. A noise from the corner of the hut drew his attention before he could recheck the coordinates of the mountain opium base.

Hook was field-stripping and cleaning Kabrina's Kalashnikov rifle. Whatever the quality of the terrorist training Hook had received, he must have been a good pupil. He definitely knew what he was doing.

Bolan went back to the map. Going it alone meant taking a risk, sure. But this whole mission was one big risk from the start.

Hook could help. Even if they had no words in common, he could give directions that Bolan would understand. Sure, it would be dangerous for the little Turk. But he was one man, against, possibly, the welfare of an entire nation.

But Mack Bolan did not weigh a good man's life against another's. Mack Bolan did not play God.

He would stick to the game plan he had always used: intelligence, analysis, and decision.

And as far as it was humanly possible, he would risk no person's life but his own.

Kabrina touched his arm, and Bolan was reminded

of how much he had already drawn this unusual woman into his mission. The only way he could assure that she was in no danger was to get away from her, as quickly as possible.

Bolan had long since come to grips with the fact that his very presence could put people in the enemy's gunsights. The partings were no easier than they had ever been, but they were a responsibility.

"Come outside with me," Kabrina said.

"I don't have much time, Kabrina," Bolan said gently. "That dope could start to move down the mountain at any time, and before it does, I've got to be there."

"I understand. But give me three minutes."

He couldn't deny her that, she who had already given so much herself.

The mother and grandmother were standing where Bolan had first seen them. They stared darkly at him as he came out of the hut into the bright spring sunshine. Kabrina said something to them in a gentle voice. Her mother gazed at her, then nodded, her eyes softening.

"I told her you are a good man," Kabrina said.

Bolan looked down at this woman who had come through so much. His eyes traveled past the fine-featured face to take in the lush curves below. Her hand on his arm felt warm.

"Who are you?" she said.

Bolan met her gaze, then shook his head slowly.

"I'm sorry," she said. "I'm frightened, and I don't know why. You're going to take care of this, I know, and it will be all right."

Bolan waited. The girl hesitated, as if she were trying to decide something.

"You are a good man, whoever you are," she said finally.

Bolan looked away down the grassy plain of the hill, just starting to turn green under the gentle hand of spring, sweeping down to the stream and then rolling away over the hill opposite. The only sound was the soft whisper of the breeze.

But even that wind spoke of war. There had been battles here through the ages, harsh native clashes between many peoples. Bolan could almost hear the thud of bronze sword on stretched-hide armor, the hoarse shouts of the commanders, and the grunts of the foot soldiers who from time immemorial fought their nations' battles. In this very valley those battles raged still, perceptible only to Bolan's warrior sense: Turkmen against the ancient people of Urartu, the Ottoman Turks against the Malmuk invaders from Persia, the Kurds against the Turks, the Turks against the Armenians, all here in this land in the shadow of Mount Ararat.

If they had not been good wars (was there ever truly a good war?), they were wars of conviction, often for a homeland. Yeah, a homeland. That key word that held so much meaning for Marko Adamian and this woman, Kabrina. One had seen his wrested from his people; the other was fighting to see that the same thing did not happen to hers. Homeland: a concept of value and, sure, a word worth fighting for.

Kabrina took his arm again and led him toward the stand of cypress trees beside the small stream rolling down the slope, swollen now with the spring melt of high-mountain snow.

"I want to help," the girl said suddenly.

"You've helped already."

"I can help you find that base. I've been all through this country with my family, looking for pasture in the summer, for shelter in the winter. I know it, and I can help guide you."

"No."

The girl looked up at him, pleading in her eyes. Bolan wanted to take her in his arms, to hold her, to let her know it was all right.

"I understand what is at stake for you," she said

softly. "Don't forget I was educated in your country. If these people succeed, I can see how it will tear apart the Middle East and set American policy back for years. I also know what drugs can do to a society. For decades opium addiction permeated this country.

"But you must understand what is at stake for me," she went on. "This land has been torn by battle for thousands of years. If I am committed to my country and my people, I must do all in my power to see that we survive and prosper, and not by growing the death flower for those men on the mountain. Surely that is something a man like you understands."

"I do understand, Kabrina." But how could he explain to this girl the torment behind his decision to stalk the hellground alone? He had suffered too many times in the past when he had allowed people to walk beside him in battle. Yeah, battle meant casualties; death was an inseparable part of warfare, and those who insisted on carrying Mack Bolan's standard knew what they were getting into, and had died as largely as they lived. And yet....

Seven of Bolan's comrades from the war in Vietnam, members of his Death Squad, had given their lives to his cause in the first Los Angeles campaign. There had been Margarita, the fiercely anti-Castro Cuban refugee who had become his ally in Miami, only to die a hellishly torturous death in reward for her loyalty. Later, in New York, the petite and lovely Evie Clifford had suffered the same ghastly fate, reduced to a quivering mass of screaming nerve endings, crying out for the Mafia "turkey doctor" to end it all with the mercy of death, her only crime the succor she and her roommates had given Mack Bolan during a period of forced convalescence.

There were others, more than Mack Bolan preferred to think about. His hand had been the instrument of death for countless Mafiosi without whom the world had become a better place. But his touch had also led to the end of a few fine and selfless men and women, whose loss made that same world infinitely poorer.

This was a new war, sure, but the risks were the same, risks that he could not take the slightest chance of inflicting on this woman whom he had met just an hour before, but who had already shown herself to be an extraordinary ally.

Kabrina was saying something else, pressing her point, when Bolan spotted the Turk....

He was on the other side of the little stand of cypress trees, carefully threading his way toward them. He was so intent on avoiding every twig, on making no noise, that he was not even looking up.

Kabrina saw Bolan reach for the Beretta, and she cut herself off in mid-sentence. The sudden silence made the Turk gunner look up too—just in time to catch a 9mm jacketed slug that plowed into the bridge of his nose and on through his skull to take off most of the top of his head in a gory spray of gray and white and red.

Kabrina dropped to her knees, but she did not scream.

Bolan moved through the trees to the man, stepping quickly, but alert to any others who might be lurking in the woods. He grabbed up the Kalashnikov and ripped two spare clips from the terrorist's belt.

The girl seemed all right. Her face was white and drawn, and she was trembling slightly, but she wasn't on the verge of hysteria.

Bolan came back with the rifle and with one hand pulled her roughly to her feet.

A small rise separated them from the stone hut. Hook was standing atop it, waving them toward him and then pointing toward the valley floor. Bolan and the girl topped the rise and followed Hook's gesture.

A dozen men, each armed like the one Bolan had just killed, were standing next to two unmarked Jeeps and a Land Rover.

They wore the same uniform that the men in Hook's convoy had.

Damn, Bolan thought. He looked at the little Turk and the girl beside him, who suddenly had become caught in the crossfire of his fight, their only crime the assistance they had given him.

Okay, but there was no point now in thinking about what might have happened before, only in what was about to happen now.

Mack Bolan had plenty of experience in playing it by ear, and plenty in playing it by the numbers.

He preferred playing it by the numbers, but this time the ear had it.

Had the numbers just about run out?

17

Sirhan Takim knew that the man called Paradine was wrong. He most certainly was not a coward.

It was true that everything he had gained was at the expense of other men's losses, but that was the way of the world. Survival went to the fittest, but the converse was true as well. Those unfit did not survive, and no one, certainly not Takim, would mourn them.

Takim was a fit survivor.

He grew to puberty in the slums of Ankara, never knowing his father, abandoned by his mother almost before he had learned to talk. Surrounded by the desperate poverty of his environment, he turned it to his advantage, by learning to prey on the misery of others. This was his first lesson of life, and he embraced it wholeheartedly.

Takim progressed rapidly from begging to picking pockets, mugging, and burglary. He killed his first man when he was eleven, striking him from behind with a piece of masonry in order to steal his purse. The purse contained 500 lira—the equivalent of about twenty dollars.

By his teenage years he had refined his skills to a fine art.

The group of thugs and common criminals he joined at that time happened to call itself the Army of the Revolutionary Left. Takim could not have cared less about the ARL's politics. He was simply glad to have found a home for his violent skills.

He added to his repertoire the art of bullying and rose rapidly up through the ranks. Suddenly he had what had always been denied him: warm food, clothing, a billet, money. And one thing more.

Power.

Power to control. Power that thrived on the fearful respect of his subordinates. Power for its own sake.

Takim made himself a colonel. When he gained the seat of the government in Ankara, he planned to make himself a general.

There was only one thing that stood between the so-called Colonel Takim and the destiny he saw as his rightful due.

One blacksuited infidel devil-dog in that stone hut above him.

One man could never stop Takim. One man *would* never stop him.

For just a moment, Takim wondered about the single gunman he had sent up ahead. Takim had ordered the man to reconnoiter. He had then taken him aside and made it clear that wealth and fame would belong to the man if he happened to kill the one in the blacksuit.

The man should have returned. Or at least Takim should have heard the sound of gunfire. No doubt he was simply being cautious. That was fine. Takim considered caution a great virtue.

The caution of sending other men to do his fighting for him had saved Takim from death several times in his life.

Takim put these thoughts from his mind. He would concentrate on nothing but the infidel's death until it was accomplished.

And accomplish it he would. Because if he did not, Takim knew with all the certainty of his Islamic faith, he was a dead man.

From a tactical point of view, Bolan realized, a defensive stand was the best reaction. The stone hut could weather anything short of a direct grenade hit, and the terrorists had to advance over close to 200 meters of open ground, moving uphill at that.

But there were noncombatants in that hut with him, three women whose only crime consisted of aiding him when he needed aid the most.

So suddenly Mack Bolan's war had become personal again.

The big stakes, the consequences of losing this one, had not changed. A heroin flood that could tear America apart at the seams. The terrorist overthrow of a crucial Middle East ally. An international incident involving two influential Americans. Bolan had not lost sight of any of that.

But now he also bore the responsibility for three innocent women, and at this moment that was just as important. Bolan knew what would happen if he did not stop those men below, he could imagine how they would use Kabrina and her mother and even her grandmother. Death, when it finally came, would be a blessing.

Bolan shook that one out of his mind. It would not happen, not while he lived.

He sat the women on the bench against the back wall, as far away from the door as possible. Kabrina was explaining to the two older women that they must not move from the bench, no matter what happened. They nodded in unison, the same impassive expression masking whatever their thoughts were.

The numbers were tight, but the blitzing fighter figured he had a few left. The main attack force would wait a few minutes, either for the return of the man with his report, or for the sound of gunfire, which would indicate that the fight had been made for them already. Bolan checked the banana clip on the AK-47 he had taken from the Turk gunner. It was full, and he jammed it back home. His other weapons were already in position. An HE grenade came out of one of the slit pockets of the blacksuit and found a home in the breech of the M203 launcher attached to the '16.

Hook came up beside him. Kabrina's AK-47 was cradled in his arms.

"He wants to fight beside you," Kabrina translated from her place on the bench. "He says he is no coward."

The little Turk nodded solemnly. Bolan knew that what he said was true. It was not cowardice that had made him throw down his weapon in the first firefight on the grassy plane. It was despair and disgust at having to fight for a cause he knew was wrong.

Now he had found one he believed to be right, and he wanted Bolan to give him a chance. A chance to be a man.

Okay, Bolan would give it to him. The team rosters were going to have to change now. Bolan could no longer afford to keep the little Turk out of it if the women were to be protected.

"Tell him to stay here," Bolan said to Kabrina. "His assignment is to protect you at all costs."

"What are you going to do?" Kabrina asked.

Bolan stood up. He clipped the Ingram to the cord hanging from his neck, patted the handguns at hip and arm, and picked up the M-16.

"I'm going to take their fight to them," Bolan told the girl. "And I'm going to shove it right back down their throats."

The point man never knew what hit him.

One moment the Turk was standing in front of the Jeep on which the heavy-barrel .50-caliber machine gun was tripod-mounted. The next moment a 9mm steel-jacket punched into his face, courtesy of the silenced Beretta Brigadier in Bolan's right hand.

The two men at the gun stared down stupidly at their comrade. Their brains were struggling to figure out how the man's face had silently dissolved into a gaping red hole.

The next silent bone-cruncher caught the belt man in the side of the head. Blood splattered on the gunner, who then tried to bring the machine gun around when Bolan's third round tore a ragged hole in his throat.

Bolan then put a slug into each of the two front tires. Up on the hill, the remaining ten men were advancing in a wide line toward the stone hut. At one end of the line, Bolan recognized the red beret and the gait of the one who had led the convoy, besides Hook, one of only two survivors of that hellrain. The Turks were within fifty meters of the hut.

The numbers had been tight to start with, and they were getting tighter. Through the window at the hut's rear, around the cypress, a double-time duckwalk down the cover of the hillside stream bed, and Bolan was at the enemy's rear. But the numbers were clicking away as he mopped up the gun crew.

Just then the numbers went to hell.

Some combat instinct made one of the advancing troops turn to check his rear guard. Bolan had already picked this man out when he glimpsed the line on his way down to back-door it. He was bigger than the Turks, and instead of the khaki uniform, he wore green fatigues. Something about him said "warrior" to Bolan.

The big man in green shouted an order. There was momentary confusion. The terrorist troops stopped and turned in a ragged formation, suddenly aware that something had gone wrong behind them.

It took only that moment for Bolan to drop to a crouch, cradle the grenade launcher, and lob a 40mm can of high explosive right into the middle of the line.

Bolan darted toward the Rover as the grenade hit home. He dived behind the wheel, stabbed the starter with his foot, and turned the all-terrain rig straight up the hill in a death-charge into the enemy's maw.

The Rover bucked across the stream, hung for a second on the opposite bank, and then the all-weather tires bit into the grass, and the rig hurtled up the hill. Bolan aimed it at where the grenade had struck, the dust and smoke starting to blow clear. Three bodies littered the grass. One was missing its head; another had a crater-shaped hole gouged out of the middle of its chest.

The third had taken the direct hit. It was just bits and pieces of what had once been a man.

A Turk rose to Bolan's left and raised his rifle. Bolan yanked the wheel over hard and felt the solid *whomp* as the fender of the Rover caught the man. There was a bump and the unmistakable sound of bones being crushed to shards as the rig rocked over the guy's body.

Bolan jerked the wheel back over to the right. The low-range four-wheel-drive transmission whined as Bolan down-shifted and punched the accelerator to the floorboards.

A slug cut a hole in the windshield and sliced a chunk out of Bolan's right shoulder. He jerked the Ingram from its lanyard, transferred it to his left hand, and kicked open the driver's side door, leaning out behind it and steering from instinct with his right hand.

The Turk rifleman's burst continued to track across the front of the rig, searching for the black-clad driver. A moment later, the gunner found what he was looking for when a four-shot grouping from the Ingram stitched across his chest.

Then the Rover coughed and died, steam pluming from its perforated radiator. Bolan rolled out the door and came up behind the cover of the disabled rig.

The rear attack had taken some of the punch out of the terrorist assault. But there were five of them left, including the big man in green. And they had gained the lip of the little flat spot on the hillside that was the stone hut's yard, too close to the building for Bolan to risk another grenade.

One part of Bolan's combat mind noted that the Turkish commander was nowhere in sight.

For the moment they had Bolan pinned down behind the Rover, and the battleground was suddenly, glaringly quiet. Bolan gathered his feet under him, ready to charge them before they charged the hut.

There was no time to think defense or strategy. A head-on assault was the only thing that could protect the three women.

Then the ratcheting chatter of a thirty-round AK-47 clip being emptied on full automatic split the silence. Bolan stood in time to see Hook moving forward from the door of the hut as the last of the 7.62mm screamers from his chattergun tore into the line of gunmen. The little Turk spun and scampered past the hut toward the cover of the trees beyond it.

He almost made it. He was two steps from that cover when he was hit.

But Bolan was not waiting to see where Hook got it. The diversion was all that he needed. He dumped the M-16; he could no longer afford the extra weight if he was going to get to the women.

Hook's rapid-fire burst had taken out three of the Turks. The last soldier raised up to sight in on the charging black-clad blitzer and took the rest of the Ingram's clip full in the face. His head exploded off his shoulders.

Bolan spun on his heel, and for one moment of eternity, time seemed to stop dead.

Every detail of that tiny yard stood out in stark relief. The shredded bodies of the dead terrorists littered the ground at his feet. Ten meters to his left, Hook lay motionless.

And ten meters to his right, the big man in green

stood facing him, his AK-47 in one hand, a full magazine in the other.

A split second later, and the man would have reloaded.

"Drop it," Bolan snapped.

The man stared at him, and in that look was not the fanatical fervor of the Turkish terrorists, but something even more terrible. It was naked viciousness, the look of a man for whom killing needed no cause, a man for whom the rank stench of spilled blood was cause enough.

Then he did drop the empty Kalashnikov, and his right hand slapped at the .45 automatic riding his hip. But the big silver AutoMag was already clearing leather and coming up level in Mack Bolan's hand.

The 240-grain hollow-point flesh-shredder slammed into the man's face at more than 1,400 feet per second. And eternity opened wide for the professional killer named Karel.

That left the Turkish commander.

Even as he sprinted for the hut, it passed through Bolan's mind that the terrorist leader may have long ago fled the carnage. He had already shown his cowardly stripe during their first engagement. But that wasn't something Bolan was betting his life on.

Bolan kicked open the door of the hut and slammed his body back against the wall. When no fire came, he stepped into the room.

The two women stared at him. For once their eyes were wide with emotion, and the emotion was fear.

There was no sign of the Turkish leader.

And there was no sign of Kabrina.

As he turned for the door, Bolan heard the whine of a motor, distant and throaty. He got to the edge of the yard in time to see the Turk commander's Rover careen down the road.

It had already covered at least a hundred meters, but he could still make out the Turkish leader in the driver's seat, and a white blouse and the dark mane of Kabrina's shiny hair marked where she lay slumped in the back of the Jeep.

Bolan swore. He had played it by the numbers, right down the line. Hook had fulfilled his assignment as well. Without his counterassault, the whole thing might have gone to hell.

But damn it, they had the girl. The one person who never deserved to be a part of any of this, and now she was in the hands of the vicious, mindless bastards.

A personal war, for sure. Just as it had always been.

Mack Bolan was going to show them what a personal war really meant.

18

"Kill her," Paradine said.

"What?"

"Kill the woman. A life for a life."

"I don't think...."

"No, you don't think," Paradine snapped. "So help me, Takim, I will have her life in vengeance, or just as I swore, I will have yours."

Takim frowned. He felt quite calm and unafraid, which surprised him a bit. But he knew that once again he had gone against the devil infidel in the suit as black as dark night, and he had returned to tell about it. True, many men had died. But what were the lives of a dozen men to Colonel Takim? There were more where they had come from, and more waiting behind them. Takim was a past master at exploiting desperation.

Of them all, only Takim came back alive. That alone was enough to strengthen him, to convince him that the special providence of Allah was upon him. And that was why the fuming and ranting by the big blond infidel no longer had the effect of cowing Takim. He looked up with what was almost serenity as the man in dark glasses stormed back and forth across the small hut he had appropriated for his private billet.

"Because of you, Takim, a good man died," Paradine was saying. His voice was low, but it trembled with barely controlled rage. "*You* are the murderer of Karel, Takim. He was a man, worth ten of those stupid cows out there whom you call soldiers." His voice rose. "He was a warrior, Takim, not a snivelling, cowardly son of a mongrel dog like you."

The blond man's voice choked off, almost as if he were weeping, but his eyes remained hidden behind the black shades. If the other hardman, who stood to the side with his autorifle at parade rest, felt any emotion at this discussion of his fallen partner, he did not reveal it in his expression.

Paradine turned suddenly and slammed his fist down on the table. "Kill her!" Paradine said again. "Kill her, or as God is my witness, I will kill you."

Takim cleared his throat. There was no reason for the girl to die—not when Takim could think of a much better use for her. As they drove back toward the base, he had not failed to notice her full breasts and the flowing lines of her thighs, which even the peasant garb could not hide. When he stopped the Jeep, and then ordered her to pull up her skirt so he could see her long legs, she had called him a filthy name. That had only served to fire up his blood. Later, when he was rid of the sound of this stupid Paradine's voice, Takim would find out if the rumors about the hot-blooded Kurdish women were true.

Takim stood up and put both hands on the table, staring at Paradine with a steady gaze. "I am in charge, Paradine," he said evenly. "You are here in an advisory capacity only, and it is time you started to realize that." Takim almost surprised himself with the note of deadly calm in his voice, but it was time that this man understood who led the Turkish Peoples' Liberation Army. The gunman at the door clearly recognized the threat in Takim's tone. He took a step forward, and his knuckles whitened where he held his rifle.

"Listen to me, Paradine," Takim said flatly. "I am sorry that your man died. But it could not be helped." In one way, at least, the massacre at the stone hut had worked to Takim's advantage. There was no one alive to reveal that Takim had fled with the woman and left Karel to meet his death. "What we must do now is work together. The operation must be saved, and that must be everyone's first priority."

"That is correct," Paradine said, his voice just as hard. "But understand this, Takim—your Russian friends would like to see you succeed, and I am here to see that you do. But I am not working for you; I am working for the best interests of Moscow. Right now, I agree. We must unite against the common enemy, and we must fight as brothers." Paradine paused. "But I would suggest, Takim, that you continue to endeavor to reassure me of the wisdom of our alliance."

Takim shook away the clammy touch of the unspoken threat. No longer would he be cowed by this infidel mercenary.

"For all we know," Paradine said, "you could have led our enemy right to the perimeter of our camp."

"No," Takim interrupted. "There was no time for him to follow. Both of the remaining vehicles were disabled. Besides, I checked behind me and took suitable precautions. I am not stupid," he added disdainfully.

"The little Turk, Horuk."

"The little Turk is dead," Takim said coldly. "I killed him with my own hand." The lie came easily. "The man in black is no longer a threat."

Paradine stared icily at Takim. The Turkish colonel noticed that his hands were clenching and unclenching involuntarily. "He is no longer a threat when he is dead, and his bleeding head is in my hands," Paradine said. "You don't know this man, Takim. Your so-called revolution would not know a real man if he came up and pissed on your shoes. But I know him."

Paradine's voice was very low now, almost expressionless. It was as if a cold, damp finger was drawing a line down Takim's spine, but he willed himself to show no fear.

"He is Death, Takim," Paradine said. "Death in black, behind you, around you, never in front of you. But he is not some spirit, some ghost of retribution. He is a single man, flesh and blood and bone like you and me. The bullet will tear through his skull and brain just as easily as any other man's, Takim."

Paradine reached inside his Windbreaker, took out the Luger, and checked the action.

"My bullet, Takim," he said quietly.

Takim was no stranger to bloodlust, but never had he seen anything to match the blond man's fervor. But taken too far, he knew that even fervor could be dangerous.

"What of the mission?" Takim said quickly.

Paradine seemed to snap out of a trance. "Of course," he said. "We must move out immediately. The first two buses are loaded. This time we will not fail. We have already lost nearly forty men, including Karel, as well as several vehicles and our most important armaments—among them," he added viciously, "our heavy machine guns, which you saw fit to abandon."

Takim let the remark pass. He waited calmly for the blond man to finish.

"Form a squad of twenty men to accompany the buses," Paradine said. "And prepare the Armenians for travel. This place is no longer safe, and they may ultimately be our most valuable asset." Paradine stared at Takim, the dark lenses of his glasses like the portals of Hell. "This time there must be no mistake."

"I tell you," Takim said, his voice steady and commanding, "there is no need for panic. He cannot find us. I left no trail. The little Turk is dead, and without the girl he is lost."

"Yes, the girl," Paradine said. "What possessed you to bring her here?"

"Don't be stupid," Takim said. The gunman near the door frowned at him, and Paradine stiffened, but Takim did not move. The blond man must know that Takim was not afraid of him. "She can be of great value to us. She is a hostage, and should it become necessary, we may exchange her for one of our people, or use the threat of her death as a tool for negotiation." Takim grinned slyly. "We may even stage a little drama to make it appear that your Armenians killed her. That would fit into your plan, would it not?"

"Go on," Paradine ordered.

"She is also valuable right now," Takim said. "She can tell us more about this man in black and how much he knows, if any others are about to arrive to threaten our operation, and all sorts of interesting intelligence. I can assure you she will cooperate with the interrogation." Takim grinned again, but this time his expression was lewd. "I shall conduct the questioning myself."

"Very well," Paradine said. "I await your report."

Takim nodded curtly and turned on his heels. He neither hesitated nor hastened, and a moment later, outside in the warm spring sunshine, he could feel the strength and confidence pounding in his veins.

Richard Hagen turned from the dirty window of the shack and frowned into the semidarkness of the small room. Something was going down, but Hagen was damned if he could figure out what.

Hagen was no longer preoccupied with the absurdity of the situation, the suddenness of his transfer from a warm bed in Georgetown to a rough wooden shack in eastern Turkey. That was behind him; nothing mattered now but the here and the now. The why could be sorted out later.

Sure, Hagen was no warrior. But he was a survivor. He had survived the political wars, the accusations of corruption that any man in his position faced sometime in his career, the thousand petty skirmishes. All of his professional life had been a hard-fought battle, and the stakes were always political life or death.

Now the stakes were *actual* life or death. It was a different kind of fight than the ones Hagen knew well, but it wasn't one he was planning to lose. He had no plan, no weapons, and no special reason for hope. But he had one thing: the conviction that this was not his time to die, and the resolution to back that up with whatever strength he could muster.

Richard V. Hagen was a sticker.

He checked the scene in the center of the compound again. Troops were loading crates into the rear of one of the old buses, the back seats of which had been removed. They were in a hurry. One man dropped a crate, and the one they called Colonel Takim turned red in the face and screamed at him.

He turned away. It was time to wake Adamian up and tell him about the girl Hagen had seen them bring in, and the look on Takim's face, fear and rage and relief and satisfaction all mixed in together, when he had come back without the men he left with. Maybe Adamian could make sense of it. All Hagen could figure was that Takim had either abandoned his squad or lost them in a skirmish. Hagen hoped it was the latter. If it was, and if their luck were holding, that skirmish was with their friend in black.

They'd have to stay alert at all times. Hagen had no idea what was coming, but he knew there wouldn't be a whole lot of warning.

Then the door of the shack flew open. Adamian sat up quickly on the bed, instantly awake, peering at the three guards who burst in.

The next moment the guards were manhandling the two men out of the room, half dragging them across the compound. No one had a chance to say a word.

Hagen's heart sank. They were being taken out of the compound. And that meant they'd be that much harder to find.

Assuming anyone was looking.

Paradine watched from the porch of his shack as the two Armenians were taken across the compound. Halfway across, the big one, Adamian, pulled his arm from the grip of his guard, stared at the man haughtily, and then continued on toward the bus under his own power.

At the rear of the second bus, Takim was supervising the loading of the crates of raw opium, although "supervising" was hardly the correct word. What a pompous little idiot, Paradine thought. What he seemed to be doing at the moment was berating his men with trite obscenities, countermanding the orders of his lieutenants, and getting in the way.

As stupid and ineffectual as the Turk was, Paradine knew he could be dangerous. He had the ferret-like cunning of a coward and the morals of a street whore, backed by the instinct for survival and self-aggrandizement that had brought him as far as he had progressed.

Dangerous, most likely. Expendable, most assuredly. The opium operation was nearing a successful completion. And there were any number of self-styled revolutionaries who would be happy to serve as Moscow's puppet in the new government in place of Takim.

Inside the shack the hardman was oiling the barrel of his Kalashnikov. He looked up as Paradine came into the room.

"I believe, Tor," Paradine said, "that after all the opium has been transferred, Takim will no longer be of much use to us."

Tor's eyes flashed a question.

"After the last load leaves the camp," Paradine said, "eliminate him. Do it quietly, without alerting the camp. It is not necessary that I be made aware of the particular time or circumstances."

Tor put away the gun rag and snapped the sling back onto the rifle.

"Don't give it another thought," he said.

19

When Bolan came back into the stone hut, Hook was talking to the two women, the mother and grandmother, in a low voice. On Bolan's entrance he nodded solemnly toward the big man, then laid a gentle hand on the older woman's knee.

Hook's face was a pale gray white, and his hand trembled slightly. He had probably suffered a concussion, but he had still been damn lucky. Karel's bullet had cut a shallow two-inch groove along Hook's right temple, just laying bare the white of the bone. A fraction of an inch to the left, and the 86-grain slug would have fractured the little Turk's skull like an eggshell. A fraction of an inch farther, and the guy's brains would have been scrambled.

Bolan cleaned the wound, then took antibiotic powder, disinfectant, and a compress from a slit-pocket, and dressed the cut. Hook was running a slight fever, but on balance the guy was in pretty good shape.

Then Bolan turned his attention to his own wound. He dressed the slashed skin in a few seconds, wincing slightly from the sting of the alcohol but otherwise unaffected by what had happened to him.

He couldn't say the same thing for the Rover. It sat where he'd abandoned it, three-quarters of the way up the hill. The 7.62x39mm pounders had torn the hell out of the radiator and engine block.

The two Jeeps that the Turks had come in sat at the foot of the slope. The second one, the one he had disabled via a 9mm puncture in each of the front tires, interested Bolan the most. In his haste to escape with the girl, Takim had not even thought to chuck a grenade into the rig. It was a mistake that Bolan would see that he paid for, in spades. But right now the Jeep and its contents were Bolan's, spoils of war.

Some pretty fair spoils, too. The gun in the back of the rig was a Goryunov SGM, a tripod-mounted heavy machine gun that was a newer version of a Soviet weapon that was introduced during World War II, the SG43. Spitting 650 rounds of lethal 7.62x54mm bone-crushers a minute, at a muzzle velocity of nearly 3,000 feet per second, the Goryunov was the elite of Russian small arms. It was fed by a 250-round belt magazine coiled in a metal box, and there were several of these in the back of the Jeep as well.

It took Bolan less than fifteen minutes to strip the two front tires from the first Jeep in line and mount them on the gunship. He siphoned gas from the first rig to the second, then quickly checked out its systems and ascertained all was go.

Hook was still talking quietly to the women, and again he gestured at Bolan. The big man realized that the little Turk was reassuring them, telling them that Bolan would bring Kabrina back to them. The two women stared up at him in stony silence, their eyes dark with accusation.

Bolan didn't blame them. Hours before, they were living a quiet pastoral life in these beautiful mountains, warmed by the early spring sun, waiting patiently for their men to return from the high country. Now that life had been ripped into a thousand tattered pieces. Mack Bolan had turned their rustic home into a living hellground, and with the loss of their only child, they had been caught in the crossfire.

Yeah, crossfire. Renegade Turks on one side, backed by the Kremlin and armed with a plan to turn tens of thousands of Americans into heroin-deadened shells. On the other side, the prestige of the United States and stability in the volatile Middle East. And in the middle, some misguided Armenians, blinded by an understandable nationalism, but caught up in something they could not possibly fight their way out of alone.

Behind it all, a movement based on a lie: international terrorism, which existed on the corrupt premise that animal force was superior to moral right.

They didn't care whom they used, whom they double-crossed to achieve their twisted goals. Kabrina, Hook, Adamian, Hagen, even Takim, all pawns of some sort in the vicious game. Crossfire, sure. Double crossfire. And one man standing alone to stop it from happening.

No, damn it, that wasn't right at all.

Bolan was not alone. People were with him, all around him, and he took strength from their spirit.

Lots of people. The tens of thousands who would be bound up in the vicious chains of drug addiction. The good people of Turkey, who would surely be oppressed by the so-called revolutionaries whose only cause was to exploit this crucial country for their own enrichment and lust for power. And the good people of his own country, free and true men and women everywhere, the people for whom Mack Bolan had committed himself to war everlasting against Animal Man, wherever he was.

No, Bolan told himself, *he* had not turned these people's home into a hellground. But those who did were going to pay for it, pay with their blood.

God help them if they harmed the girl. Bolan would see their souls roasting in hell. A man-made hell that would leave them screaming for the mercy that they had never granted anyone else.

That was a pledge the savages could rely on.

Hook stood up. He swayed and a grimace of pain crossed his face, but then he stood erect. The game little Turk slung Kabrina's Kalashnikov over his shoulder and spoke a few words of farewell to the women.

The balance had tipped the other way now. Kabrina's life was at stake and there was no way Bolan could complete his mission without the little Turk's help. Hook's directions were the only way Bolan could be sure of finding the terrorist base.

Bolan gathered up his own weapons and nodded a goodbye to the women, meeting their accusing gaze with an expression of quiet confidence.

"I'll bring her back," he said. Kabrina's mother stared at him, then nodded, as if she understood.

Outside, Hook was gesturing impatiently for Bolan to follow him to the Jeep. It was time to go.

And time for the payoff too. Bolan knew he owed a large debt to Kabrina, and now to this young Turkish castaway who had grown into a man before Bolan's eyes.

Bolan smiled grimly and followed Hook down the hill.

20

By the time they reached the high mountain country, Bolan had worked out enough gestures so that he and Hook could communicate a little. When the little Turk pointed Bolan up a fork to the right of the main dirt road along the river, he understood that this was the final approach route, and that they were about a half-hour from the terrorist base camp.

Hook closed his eyes, now deep-sunk with the pain that the bumpy ride had to be causing him, and dozed off. Bolan hoped the little guy would make it.

They had come about a hundred kilometers so far. The road along the river was rugged, but this road up the mountain was little more than a trail. The Jeep whined in low-low as it scrambled up the steep incline. The road had been graded recently, but the spring melt-off had carved a contour map of ruts and washouts into it. Each time the rig took a particularly hard lurch, Hook grunted in his sleep.

They were in the Kara River country, and the road wound its way into the rugged, mountainous terrain of the river's south watershed. It was early evening, and shadows were long across the road, although above them the sun still colored the high ridge. Bolan estimated less than an hour to darkness.

The top of the ridge was about 1,500 meters above them. According to Hook's sketch, the mine was 500 meters below the summit on the other side of the ridge, where the slope was gentler. On this side, the mountain rose at an angle of close to forty degrees, and the road was now a series of long switchbacks hugging the steep grade.

Bolan pulled over to the inside edge of the road and got out. An infrared monocle came from a slit-pocket in the thigh of the blacksuit. From the far outside edge of the road, he could see most of the mountainside above.

And yeah, there was something to see, all right. Two buses, three switchbacks above, slowly feeling their way down the mountain.

There was no room to maneuver for position, and there was no time to pick a battleground of Bolan's choosing. The road was barely wide enough for the Jeep to turn around in, and even that would take some jockeying.

But that meant that the buses could not turn around at all.

This leg of the switchback was about 300 meters long. The Jeep was parked fifty meters from the upper end. That was just about right. The steepness of the terrain, the thick brush covering the slope, and the Jeep's position snug up against the mountainside would hide the rig from the view of anyone above. Especially anyone concentrating on piloting an unwieldy bus down the narrow trail.

The element of surprise was Bolan's. The lead bus would not spot them until it was nearly on top of them.

It was hard-blitz time—hit and git. He had to clear the road in front of them as quickly as possible.

The real objective was that base at the abandoned mine, and the cache of narcotics that had to be destroyed.

And there was also a girl, a girl who was willing to give her life for Mack Bolan.

It was a life the icy-eyed man was not yet ready to accept.

But now it was a matter of first things first. The ETA for the bus was less than a minute away.

Hook was standing in the Jeep's open rear deck, positioning the first cartridge of the ammo belt in the feedway of the Goryunov. The little Turk yanked back on the dual handles at the end of the stocks, and the first round clicked home. Hook nodded his readiness.

Bolan had just enough time to grab the M-16/203 rifle-grenade launcher combo and assume his position next to the Jeep when the first bus crept slowly around the curve ahead.

The driver was concentrating on getting the long transport around the elbow-bend, and he didn't see the deadly man in black and the armed Jeep until his back end had cleared and his front end was no more than thirty meters from the roadblock. By that time Bolan had ripped a green-and-gold HE grenade cartridge from his ammo belt and thumbed it into the launcher.

The man at the wheel looked up and gasped in surprise. He slammed his foot on the brakes, and the tires of the big converted bus locked in a dizzy skid.

The bus was still sliding down the road when the grenade plowed into it.

The front of the big rig bucked into the air, then slid precariously out over the empty space below. Men screamed with rage and fear and pain.

A moment later, the gas tank at the vehicle's rear blew the bus forward on its nose, where it teetered on the edge of the road for a moment, then pitched down the steep slope like a high diver, crashing through the underbrush with the wrenching sounds of tearing metal and the shrieks of condemned men.

The second bus had come to a sliding stop across the road. Some combat instinct made Bolan give it a quick scan with the infrared 'scope.

It was a damn good thing he did. The dark features of Marko Adamian stared at him from a window near the bus's rear.

Hook had started a strafing pass with the big SGM, the heavy 7.62mm rippers chewing through the sheet metal body of the bus as though it was paper. Bolan shouted, "No!" and cut down hard with his left arm.

The trace pattern dropped and passed just below where Adamian was pressed to the window.

The side door of the bus jerked open, and three terrorists came tumbling out. A hail of snorters from Hook's Goryunov shredded through them.

Bolan dropped a smoke grenade in front of the crippled bus and slipped over the edge of the slope. He cut through the underbrush, guiding himself by the frantic shouting of the Turks. He came up just behind its rear.

An emergency door spanned the back end of the vehicle.

Bolan tucked his legs under him and got ready to spring at the door, when it suddenly burst outward.

Marko Adamian came diving out, a Kalashnikov in his hands. Richard Hagen tumbled out on his heels.

Bolan came up over the edge of the road. Adamian swung the rifle on him, then dipped the barrel and said, "Thank God."

But Bolan knew it was too early to thank anyone.

A Turk appeared in the open rear door. Bolan zipped him from crotch to head with a burst of 5.56mm tumblers. The man toppled back into the bus. The noise of Bolan's fire was swallowed by the louder clatter of Hook's heavy artillery chewing into the front of the rig.

Bolan turned to the two men standing at the edge of the road and shoved them down the slope.

It took just two beats more to unclip a grenade from the ammo belt at his chest, yank the pin, and roll the apple down the corridor of the bus, before Bolan vaulted over the edge after the two Armenians.

The explosive went off with a dull thump, and a moment later the spilled gasoline whooshed up after it. The sky turned a dull orange red, and hunks of hot metal and torn bodies arced into the air over Bolan's head.

Bolan waited a moment for the debris to settle, then checked the roadway.

All that remained of the second bus was a bent and blackened chassis. Flames licked up lazily from the spilled pools of fuel.

Hook dipped the nose of the SGM, raised one fist in a defiant salute, and hollered something at the sky. Then he waved and grinned.

Bolan gave him a thumbs-up. Below him, Adamian and Hagen were picking themselves out of the underbrush that had stopped their descent. They started to make their way up. There didn't seem to be any broken bones.

But Bolan was no longer concerned about the two Armenians. He was a lot more interested in several million dollars' worth of crude-process opium.

And one even more valuable girl.

With satisfaction, Sirhan Takim watched the two buses pass through the gates of the compound. The first load was on its way. It would come back to him in the form of the financing that would insure the success of his revolution, the revolution that would install Takim as the ruler of all of Turkey.

With his victory would come power. Power to command, power to control, and the power of sweet vengeance. The people who had lorded it over him, the people who had condemned him to a life of poverty—they would feel that power when Takim ruled.

Takim had no ideological objection to poverty. Indeed, he would be quite happy to see most of his subjects live in abject degradation. Poor people were weak people, and weak people were the easiest to control.

And control them Takim would, while living in the lap of utter luxury.

Yes, it was pleasant to contemplate. But now was a time for work, not contemplation.

And Takim had a job to do that he anticipated with just as much pleasure.

A guard stood outside the door of the shack where the Kurdish woman was imprisoned. Takim dismissed him with a few curt words and waited until he had left. Then he took a ring of keys from his pocket and unlocked the padlock on the shack's door.

A cot and a chamber pot were the only furniture in the small room. The woman sat on the cot and stared at him.

There was fear in those eyes, yes. But loathing cut through that fear like a razor-sharp dagger.

Takim smiled. This one would take some taming. He would make it take a long time. It had been many weeks since he'd had a woman.

"How are you called?" Takim said.

"How are you called?" the girl mocked. "I would call you a stinking stillborn son of a pig."

Takim took two quick steps across the room and backhanded her across the face.

"If you are nice to me, I can be nice to you," Takim said, stepping back. He was breathing hard from the exertion, but more from the presence of the lush young girl. "If you are not nice to me. . . ."

He left the threat unfinished, but he could see the flicker of fear cross her eyes.

"Now," Takim said firmly. "Who is the infidel devil in black?"

The girl stared at him wordlessly.

"Where is he from?" Takim demanded. "What does he want?"

"He will kill you."

Takim grinned wolfishly. "I would not depend on that if I were you," he said. "He does not know where you are. His new comrade, the little Turk Horuk, is dead and cannot tell him. And even if by some miracle of Allah he were to find this place, he would face almost a hundred armed men. You are by yourself now, my girl, alone and abandoned. Whatever chance you have to live depends upon how nice you can be to me."

"I would rather be nice to carrion," the girl snapped.

This time Takim held himself in check. He moved quite deliberately, standing over the girl for a moment so that she was forced to look up at him. Then he reached out and grabbed a handful of the coarse fabric of her blouse.

He ripped down hard, and the material tore away. The girl caught her breath, her full breasts heaving.

By Allah, Takim blasphemed, here was something worth a revolution.

His whole body quivered in anticipation, but again he held himself in check. He would go slowly. This was something to prolong and savor.

He would learn everything the girl could tell him, and then he would take his pleasure with her as many times as he wished. Maybe he would allow one or two of his closest lieutenants to take the woman, too, while he watched.

Yet Takim was no animal.

He recognized that this girl was a magnificent object.

No doubt he would feel at least a pang of remorse when he killed her.

21

Mack Bolan had been called a lot of things in his life.

In the beginning of his one-man war, they called him a mad-dog killer. When he came home from Vietnam to Pittsfield, only to find his family destroyed by the black hand of the Mafia, and responded by visiting a fire-storm from Hell on their Unholy Thing, the liberal editorial writers and even some of the law enforcement personnel who knew firsthand of the Mob's depredations were quick to label him as an example of an already vicious man gone over the brink. He was a product of the jungle, they said, a man utterly without moral sense, a vigilante, a berserker, a man who could no longer tell the difference between right and wrong, one who lived only for the bloodlust thrill of the kill. An executioner.

It did not take long for the good people of the country to wise up. It quickly became apparent that his unique brand of warfare was having an effect without precedent in the long and frustrating war against organized crime in America: it was working. As hundreds of Mafiosi fell at his hand, the country grew and strengthened. In city after city, the Mafia and all the others who preyed on people's weaknesses descended into panic, then disarray and, finally, into eclipse. And in all those many battles, not a single innocent man or woman had died at Mack Bolan's hand.

So the glib ones, even those who were converted to sympathy for and even covert support of Bolan's crusade, came up with a new label for the man now called the Executioner. He was a Don Quixote, they decided, tilting at windmills.

He could not win, the "smart" money said. Bet on it.

For a lot of the unholy brothers of La Cosa Nostra, it was the last bet they ever made.

How, they asked, could one man hope to prevail in this impossible war?

Mack Bolan did not consider the "how." He was too busy doing, *executing*. Carrying his mission to completion. A most effective executive, indeed!

Okay, they said. This man is a tragic figure. This man has a death wish.

That one made Bolan laugh out loud. As if he had some sort of crazed compulsion to wage this war for the sake of warfare. They could not know, as he had known, the loneliness, the constant wariness, the unwanted responsibility for the life of any person whom he touched too intimately. The tension, the incredible physical demands, the fear.

Oh yeah, Mack Bolan had known fear. No sane man could have lived his life without knowing fear. But he had learned to control it, to make it work for him, just as he had adapted to all the other facets of the strange and cosmic landscape he had come to inhabit.

So no, they were wrong. He was no mad-dog killer, no Don Quixote, no death-touched tragic hero.

And he had not chosen his way of life. It had chosen him.

There were a few good people who had grown to understand. Men like Leo Turrin, who had lived just as large as Mack Bolan, maybe even larger in his own way, as an undercover fed placed deep inside the Mafia. Men like Hal Brognola, a dedicated federal cop once sworn to apprehend the blitzing Bolan, who had come to dedicate himself to a higher cause, the cause of universal right. And women, too, like April Rose, who learned that the man she loved could never be wholly hers because his love was ultimately for a greater ideal, and who learned to accept that and even share the man's deep and profound commitments.

These people understood that Mack Bolan was no more than a man, but a man who had accepted a higher calling. Right now, international terrorism was intent on sending the world on a crash course straight to Hell. Maybe Mack Bolan could stop that juggernaut course. Maybe he could slow that course a little, or make the world veer away from its ghoulish destination.

And sure, maybe it would roll right over him.

Mack Bolan didn't know.

But he did know this: there was a need, and he was a man who could fill it.

Not even the name-callers would disagree with that.

Richard Hagen stared wide-eyed at Mack Bolan, then started laughing, not loudly, just a titter of nervous release.

"Jesus," he said. "I do not believe this. Not any of it, not one bit. Not now, and not ever."

"Easy, man," Bolan said sharply. The last thing he needed was for Hagen to go hysterical.

"Sorry," Hagen said. "I'm all right. It's just...."

"Go sit in the Jeep," Bolan said. "There's a canteen on the floorboards. Relax. I've got to know some things, and fast."

Marko Adamian said, "How can I be of help?"

The big Armenian stood in the center of the dusty mountain road, his hands on hips. The khaki fatigues he wore were torn and soiled, and there were some bruises on his face where he had been beaten. There was also a fresh cut on his forehead, but it was hardly more than a scratch. Considering what he had to have gone through, Bolan thought he looked remarkably fit.

"You took quite a chance there," Bolan said.

"It was the only one we had," Adamian said. "When the machine gun fire started, all of the Turks were, shall we say, preoccupied by it. I knocked the last man in the bus over the head and took his rifle. In the confusion I don't think anyone even noticed until we were out the door. You were the only one who almost got shot."

"Thanks for holding back," Bolan said sardonically. The man's self-possession was a little grating.

"I—we—owe you a lot," Adamian said seriously.

"That can wait," Bolan said brusquely. "Right now I have to know exactly where that base is, and whether they heard the explosions."

"I doubt it," Adamian said. "The mine is on the other side of the ridge, about three miles by the road, one over country. They wouldn't have seen the flash, and there is enough mountain between us to block out the sound."

"Okay," Bolan said. "Now I'm going to need a detailed map of that road, as much as you can remember, and everything you can tell me about that base."

Adamian looked surprised. "Surely you are not going up there?"

"Look, Mr. Adamian," Bolan cut in. "I liked the way you handled yourself in Beverly Hills. I think you're basically a good man, although you've got some pretty off-beat notions about brotherhood. But I didn't come here just to save your skin."

Bolan hadn't meant to phrase it so bluntly, but there wasn't time for politeness. The next thing the big Armenian said, however, made Bolan like him a little more.

"I'll come with you," Adamian offered. "I can be of help."

"The help I need right now is any intelligence you can give me that will help me blow the top off that mountain and bring it crashing down on top of them."

But Adamian was suddenly preoccupied with something else. They had reached the Jeep. Hagen was sitting in the passenger seat, leaning back, eyes closed. Hook was standing beside the rig, and Adamian was staring at him with open hostility.

"Who is this?" Adamian demanded.

"A friend," Bolan snapped. "Meet the guy who kept those boys in the bus pinned down long enough for you to clobber one of them and get loose."

"He *is* one of them."

"He *was* one of them," Bolan corrected. "Now he's one of us."

"He's a Turk."

"Listen," Bolan said with genuine annoyance. "I don't have time for any of your crusades. This man just helped take out about two dozen of those characters, not to mention what I figure to be at least a half-million dollars' worth of high-grade opium. He also happened to save your head in the bargain."

But Bolan noticed that Hook too was staring at Adamian with barely concealed dislike. This was just what he needed: a two-man Turkish-Armenian war, while the real enemy was upstairs getting ready to unleash its terror on most of the Western world.

Maybe that was unfair, Bolan knew. The ethnic hatred between the peoples of these two men went back for centuries, and perhaps with good reason on both sides. But there was a greater threat, and it was real and it was now, and both men had to understand that, pronto.

"What about the woman?" Bolan asked, trying to snap Adamian's attention back to the matter at hand.

"What woman?"

"I saw her," Hagen put in. He was sitting up straight now, and the color was coming back into his face. "I didn't have a chance to tell you before they dragged us the hell out of there," he told Adamian. "Gimme a paper and pencil."

Bolan handed over the requested items and watched as Hagen sketched the location of the hut where he had seen them take the girl. Then Adamian took over and added some pertinent details. Hook watched the big Armenian warily and with distrust, almost as if he expected a double-cross at any moment. In general detail the finished map corresponded to the one Hook had drawn, with a few added important details as well.

It was not going to be an easy probe.

It was fully dark by now, and Bolan outlined his orders. It could only be a one-man hit, hard and fast and deadly.

All he had to do was blast a mine full of opium to kingdom-come, and come out with the girl, Kabrina.

If she was still alive.

He shook that thought out of his mind. She *had* to be alive.

"I'm going with you," Adamian said.

"No," Bolan told him. "This is my kind of fight now."

"You will need all the help you can get," Adamian insisted. "I fought for our country in the war in Korea, and not from behind a desk, either. And do not forget Beverly Hills."

Bolan had not forgotten, although it seemed hard to believe that had been only a few nights earlier. He could see the big Armenian standing coolly in the doorway of his mansion, snapping .45 caliber whizzers at the screaming attackers who were almost upon him.

"Maybe I have made some mistakes," Adamian said more quietly. "Maybe I have not known exactly who my enemy was. But those men up there...I have seen them, and they are truly evil. Perhaps I can begin to make up for...for what I helped to cause." There was a plea in his voice now. "You must let me help. For me, as well as for you and the girl."

Hook interrupted with a stream of Turkish.

"Do you understand him?" Bolan said.

"Of course. It is important to speak the language of your enemy."

Bolan let that one pass.

Adamian scowled. "He said, 'If the Armenian is to be allowed to fight beside you, so must I.' "

Okay, maybe that was the way it had to be. These two men came from backgrounds a globe apart—one from the estates of a wealthy American community, the other from the Istanbul slums—but each now faced, for the first time in his life, the chance to fight together for a greater good. Could their inherited hatred stand the test?

And one thing more: Kabrina's life was at stake, and Bolan could not afford to reject any offer of aid.

"Personally," Hagen put in, "I'd just as soon get the hell out of here." He grinned and wet his lips. "I don't suppose I could talk you boys into that proposition, could I? Okay, count me in, for whatever good I can do."

"Dikran," Adamian said solemnly, "this is your fight too. You know that."

"Oh, can it, Marko," Hagen snapped. "Let's just get the damn thing over with."

Bolan bent over the sketch spread on the hood of the Jeep, studying it, probing in his mind for its weaknesses, the places where the base could be breached. He asked a few more questions of the three men who had already been there. Then he was silent for a moment, the tactical possibilities flipping through his mind like entries on a set of index cards.

When the big, dark man straightened, his chiseled-ice features were set in a determined expression.

He outlined the plan, Adamian translating for

Hook. Then he went over it a second time, made each of them repeat his part in it, and watched for any flicker of hesitation, any sign of weakness in his own offense as he had set it out for them.

Set it out by the numbers.

Tight numbers, again. As usual.

With just one chance to make them add up.

22

There were only two guards at the gate in the chain-link fence that surrounded the mine. They were not particularly good guards. Both were far more interested in watching the frantic activity going on up near the mouth of the mine shaft than in securing their posts.

They certainly had no sense of the man in black who was hugging the shadows only a few meters from them.

The plastique explosive was already in Bolan's right hand as he knee-and-elbowed to the gate, a radio-controlled detonator already set in the goop. He slapped the hot pack softly against the base of the gate, then slithered back into the darkness. As the night swallowed him whole again, one of the guards turned and frowned at the place where Bolan had been, then shrugged to himself and went back to watching the activity at the mine.

It wasn't much of a gate—just two sections of fence mounted on hinges and chained together at the middle. A hard ram with a Jeep would breach it easily. But Bolan didn't want to just breach it.

He wanted to blast it to hell, high enough and far enough and loud enough to send a shock wave of panic rippling across the compound.

The blitzing nightfighter was in full blacksuit, hands and face blackened as well, foot tread softened in sure-grip black rubber sneakers. The silenced Beretta Belle and the booming AutoMag rode in their usual places of honor at shoulder and hip, and the Ingram machine-pistol dangled from a neck cord. The M16/203 was back at the Jeep; this was to be a soft-probe, the primary mission to liberate the girl.

After that, the real fireworks would start.

Two razor-sharp stilettos in snap-away sheathes rode on Bolan's left hip, opposite the AutoMag. A mass of ribbons criss-crossed his chest, and from them hung several nylon garrotes, as well as an extensive variety of smokers, incendiaries, and high explosives. A utility belt and the slit-pockets of the blacksuit were stocked with a variety of other handy goodies: more explosive goop, along with remote detonators and the cigarette-pack-sized transmitter that activated them, flares, penlight, and various other items.

Bolan let the dark embrace of the night envelop him as he started around the perimeter of the camp. The place was buzzing with activity. Somewhere to Bolan's right a diesel generator was chugging, and two large floodlights were bathing the mouth of the mine in their unnatural yellow glow. Two buses like the ones Bolan had stopped below, as well as a canvas-covered troop carrier, were backed up to the adit. Bare bulbs disappeared back into the cavernous mine. Men were scurrying out with wooden crates of the brown-paper-wrapped opium, struggling under the weight before dumping their loads into the truck and going back for more.

Bolan counted about forty troops in the loading detail. Another twenty or so were scattered around the compound, servicing vehicles, loading other gear, striking the tents set near the two long processing buildings. They were obviously breaking camp.

The compound was about 200 meters to a side and sloped gently away from the mine to the main gate, where the road started its steep descent. The mountain cut away steeply behind and to either side of the mine, forming a natural rear defense with flying buttresses. The rest of the perimeter was protected by the fence.

The two long processing buildings were to one side of the mine, set at right angles to the mountainside. Next to them and closer to the middle of the yard was the shack where, according to their sketch, Adamian and Hagen had been held.

And behind the two long buildings, just at the edge of the glow of the floodlights and twenty meters from the perimeter, was the shack where Hagen had seen them take Kabrina.

Bolan took a pair of insulated carbon steel cutters from a pocket and went to work on the chain-link. It took less than a minute for him to open a flap big enough to squeeze through. He bent it back into place behind him, then headed across the no-man's-land to the hut, a black shadow moving through the night he had become a living part of. A moment later he was plastered against the side of the hut, lost in the darkness.

There were two Turk hardboys guarding the door. As Bolan peered around the edge of the building, one of them gestured with his thumb toward the interior and made some crack that brought a grin from his partner. The first guard returned the chuckle, then tucked his rifle under his arm while he fished a cigarette from his pocket. The other guard struck a match and held it in cupped hands.

The first guard was drawing in the flame when something knocked the cigarette from his mouth.

He had no time to wonder about it before the sharp bite of Bolan's garrote cut through his neck flesh and severed his jugular vein.

The other man's match had not even gone out when Bolan's stiletto sliced a bubbling red ribbon across his neck.

Bolan dragged both men around to the side of the hut and dumped them in an ungainly pile. If they were uncomfortable in that position, they didn't complain.

The flimsy wooden door of the shack was fastened by a padlock. Bolan drew the silenced Beretta, slammed the sole of his foot against the wood, and barreled in behind the splintered planks.

The only light in the room came from a smoky oil lamp set on the floor. There was a cot next to it.

Kabrina lay spread-eagled on the cot, her wrists and ankles bound by ropes that ran under it. She was naked. Her blouse and skirt had been ripped away and hung from her in tatters. There was a sheen of sweat on her body, despite the chill of the night.

Colonel Takim stood above her, a wickedly curved skinning knife in his hand. He wore nothing but a pair of briefs. The rest of his clothes were scattered on the floor next to the cot.

The girl's dark eyes were glazed with fear as she turned her head to take in the black apparition that had just burst into the room.

Takim spun around. His mouth opened, but no sound came out. Out of reflex, he flung the knife in Bolan's direction. Bolan moved a half-step to one side, and the blade clattered against the wall and fell to the floor.

Whatever courage Takim had gathered to him in the past twenty-four hours dissipated like smoke, leaving only crazed panic in its place. The paralysis of his fear broke. He dropped to his knees. A babble of guttural sounds cascaded from his trembling lips, their direct meaning incomprehensible, but the high, keening sound of the abject plea for mercy came through loud and clear.

Righteous Death had just walked into Sirhan Takim's life, and he was begging Death to give that life back to him.

Mack Bolan had never despised another man so much in his life.

Takim dived to one side, scrambling desperately for the pile of clothing, pawing through it like a dog until his hand found the .45 and tore it from the flapped holster. Yet all the time he could not tear his eyes from the figure of Death Incarnate facing him implacably, and his eyes were filled with a terrible mixture of horror and hate.

The .45 had just cleared leather when the black pistol in Bolan's steady hand silently chugged a pencil of flame. A nasty red fountain exploded from between those horrified eyes, and Sirhan Takim passed from the hell of man to the hell of the gods.

Kabrina stared at the blood and gore splattered across her feet. For a moment Bolan thought she was going to scream, and sprang toward her.

Instead she stared up into his blackened face and began to weep softly with relief.

The stiletto passed through the ropes in two quick slashes. She fell into his arms, her body shuddering with all the released tension of the nightmare from which she had just been mercifully awakened.

"Are you hurt?" Bolan said gently.

"No," she said. "He didn't...he didn't have time. The other one, the blond one with the dark glasses...he told them to leave me alone.... He was going to kill me himself, I'm sure. But then this one came in and tied me...and then...." Her voice broke, and she started to sob again, pressing her body against the big man as if she wanted to melt into him.

"It's all right now," Bolan said. "But we've got to get out of here, and now."

She pushed reluctantly away from him and wiped the back of her hand across her eyes. "I'm all right now," she said, her voice almost under control.

Bolan found Takim's blouse and a light blanket among the scattered clothing and helped her into them, then took her hand and pulled her toward the door.

A Turk was standing in it, his AK-47 at port arms, staring stupidly at them.

Bolan put a silent 9mm Parabellum snorter into the now not-so-hardman. As the Turk tumbled back into the darkness, Bolan caught the falling Kalashnikov, and he and Kabrina stepped over the man's twisted, nearly headless body and moved toward the fence.

They found the other three a couple of hundred meters down from the main gate, where Bolan had left them, just around the last switchback. Bolan thrust the Russian-made rifle into Hagen's surprised hands.

"What am I supposed to do with this?" Hagen said, talking off the fear he was trying to subdue.

"You use it to protect her," Bolan snapped, his voice like brittle ice. "Just like the plan."

"I've never shot anything like this," Hagen protested.

"Just point it and pull the trigger," Bolan said. "Bang, bang, they're dead. Or you are," he added, trying to shock the man into awareness.

Hagen seemed to get the message. He took the girl by the hand.

"Good luck, man," Hagen said softly.

The girl put her hand on Bolan's arm.

Bolan grinned down at her to break the solemnity of the moment. "Take care of Mr. Hagen," he said.

Hagen and the girl started down the road to the rendezvous point. Bolan hoped to be joining them pretty quickly.

But there were a few things to take care of first.

Hook sat in the driver's seat of the armed Jeep, drumming nervously at the wheel with his fingertips, in the universal gesture of driver impatience. Adamian was in the back, double-checking the big Soviet heavy machine gun and the ammo belt feeding into it.

Bolan gave both men the thumbs-up sign, and each returned it.

"Tally-ho," Bolan said, almost to himself.

He turned and stalked back toward the hellground.

23

Paradine sat at the small desk in his hut, scowling at the Turkish-tobacco cigarette in his hand. It was giving him a headache.

A lot of what had happened in the past twenty-four hours contributed to that headache. Never had he seen such bumbling confusion, and never would he chance seeing it again. From now on, he would work only with his own hand-picked men, and he would be solely in charge. He would not suffer fools like Takim, he would not offer terms, and he would get the job done, without having his effectiveness compromised by the antics of those who were supposed to be on his side.

Paradine was a product of his time, a time in which splinter groups of international terrorism were blooming like flowers in the spring. All you needed was a few men too poor or too stupid or too desperate to know you were using them for live bait; some armament from the thriving worldwide weaponry black market; and a long, solemn-sounding name—it was best if the words *liberation* or *freedom* or *people* were part of it. Then you were all set to ravish and plunder your fellow beings.

The only gap in the scheme of international terrorism was knowledge, background, and expertise. The man called Paradine had quickly stepped in to fill that gap.

His background was cloaked in mystery. Some said he was a European; others thought he was born and brought up in Rhodesia. One unconfirmed rumor had him first surfacing during the Vietnam War, when, it was said, he fought and worked as a special free-lance advisor to the Viet Cong. On more than one occasion combat troops did report seeing a blond Occidental man with the enemy. The reliability of these sightings was never officially established, but among the grunts the stories persisted through most of the war.

Paradine was believed to have been involved in several African brush wars as a mercenary commander; in a number of terrorist offensives in the Middle East, most under contract with the PLO; and in the paid assassinations of several European and Asian politicians. Paradine himself was amused at how many actions were credited to his hand. He was fond of saying that if all the stories were true, he must be three men. This was a lie; very few of the rumors were without basis in fact.

The blond man built up a reputation and a clientele. He had no interest in a customer's politics, as long as the client could meet Paradine's fee, in advance. "Morality" was a concept with no meaning to him. And his results were guaranteed.

But these damned Turks! He had never seen such incompetence, and he planned to make it clear to his KGB contact that he would never agree to work with such again. Why, if it were not for him, Paradine shuddered to think how this operation would have turned out. Now, despite all the setbacks, he was finally bringing it to a successful conclusion. This mission would not turn out to be the first blot on his spotless record of triumphs.

The door to the hut opened, and the big hardman in green fatigues came in and stood in a pose of easy attention.

"The loading is progressing satisfactorily," the professional gun reported. "The mine should be empty within the hour. All things considered, we're looking good."

"No thanks to that stupid clown Takim."

"I'll take care of him as soon as the last load takes off. The Armenians are already on their way to. . . ." He allowed himself a grin. "To their glorious martyrdom in the cause of the Armenian homeland. Their bodies will be found, well-armed with the latest in American weapons, inside a government house in Ankara. That should please our friends across the frontier."

"Good work, Tor."

"That's what you pay for," the other said easily. "We'll be quit of the place entirely by midnight, and after that no one will be able to stop us."

"No one?" Paradine said quizzically.

"If you're thinking of the man in black," Tor said, "don't worry. He's been trouble so far, I admit, but even he wouldn't dare walk right into our midst."

Whether Paradine would have agreed with this optimistic assessment was lost in the confusion caused by the door to the hut flying open.

Paradine stood up angrily. No one but his own men was allowed to enter like that. But the Turk at the door had too much on his mind to notice the professional terrorist's annoyance.

"The woman," he panted. "She is gone. Three of the guards killed, and Takim—his brains decorate the hut."

Paradine swore and pushed the man aside. He stepped out onto the porch just in time to see the compound's gate engulfed in a billowing ball of flame. The superheated air of the shock wave rocked him back against Tor.

Men were running aimlessly toward the explosion, their guns at the ready, searching blindly for something to shoot at.

A moment later they had their target.

A Jeep came barreling through the smoke and dust of the explosion and slid to a stop just inside where the gate had been. The heavy machine gun tripod-mounted on its rear deck began to sputter flame and death.

Two hundred and fifty rounds of pounding 7.62mm tumblers tore into the line of rushing men.

Grotesque screams tearing from scorched throats were cut off in mid-holler. Bodies and parts of bodies rolled across the hellground. Blood pumped into the hard-packed, gravelly dirt and gathered in viscous pools that would not be absorbed.

Tor shouldered his AK-47 and sighted on the gunner, his finger closing on the trigger.

Before he could complete the reflex motion, there was a tremendous boom and whoosh, and the night turned into day.

A ball of roiling fire came out of the mouth of the mine, like an express train out of a tunnel.

And the ghoulish screams of burning humanity were that train's hellish whistle.

Bolan watched the sweep second hand on his chronometer go straight upright, whispered, "Now," and depressed the detonator button on the tiny transmitter.

He nodded in satisfaction as across the compound the front gate blew high into the night sky.

Men came streaming out of the mine, dropping crates as they ran. The ones at the vehicles grabbed their weapons and ran toward the chaos below.

Bolan moved from behind the rock that had been giving him cover and darted into the mouth of the mine.

A straggler came running toward him, blinking in the sudden brightness of the explosion. Bolan tracked the Ingram onto him and zipped half the clip into him in a cross-hatch pattern that turned his torso into raw meat.

It took the big, cool guy exactly forty seconds to set and arm the three hunks of "goop." As he turned and headed back the way he came, he heard the first burst from Adamian's commandeered SGM, and the echoing cries of the men who became its targets.

He came out running, gave the rest of the Ingram's magazine to two Turks whose curiosity about looking back was the last mistake they ever made, then dived to the side, behind the cover of a pile of rubble.

His thumb found the bottom of the detonator-transmitter and sent the "destruct" message back into the mine.

The flames came roaring out in answer, engulfing the nearly loaded vehicles parked at the mine's mouth. A moment later their fuel tanks went up, adding their voices to the cacophonous chorus of fiery destruction. In an instant the rigs were no more than hulks of blackened metal.

So far, right by the numbers.

Now it was time to bring the numbers home.

Bolan darted from cover and headed across the living hell that only moments before had been a terrorist compound. He stopped long enough to toss a couple of incendiaries into each of the two long processing buildings, then headed for the Jeep.

Marko Adamian had never seen anything like the guy.

An hour before, Adamian had been a prisoner in this camp, with little chance that he would ever live to tell about it. Then, when he had his chance to flee to freedom, he had chosen to go back in. Maybe he was trying to expiate what he saw as his sins. But again, deep in his heart of hearts, he had not expected to come out alive.

Now this bold man in black had turned the compound into a seething inferno, and Adamian was beginning to believe again that against all odds and rational thinking, the guy was going to get them out in one piece.

That's when the Goryunov jammed.

Maybe it was the battle pressure. Maybe his fingers had trembled just enough to betray him. But when he positioned the first cartridge of the new belt in the feedway of the big machine gun, the bolt would not relock.

Adamian looked up desperately and saw the big man in green fatigues in front of the shack, the autorifle in his hands, aiming at him....

A flash erupted from the muzzle at the instant the weapon jerked wildly into the sky. A track of autofire stitched across Tor's chest, slamming him back against the wall of the building.

Just below Adamian, the little Turk named Hook looked back, raised his AK-47 in salute, and grinned.

Hook was still grinning when the bullet hit him.

Now Paradine was tracking his Luger onto Adamian. The Armenian dropped flat to the rear deck of the Jeep beside the machine gun.

But in the pit of his gut, Adamian could already feel the deadly slap of the slug that he knew was about to finish him for good.

It happened in the space of a heartbeat. Running across the compound toward the Jeep, Bolan saw the whole drama play out before him.

He threw a shot from the Beretta at Paradine. But Bolan was running at full sprint, and the shot slammed into the boards of the shack a few inches above the blond head.

Then Bolan gained the driver's seat of the Jeep and wheeled the vehicle around toward the gate in a screeching four-wheel drift that sprayed a rooster tail of gravel behind him.

As the Jeep came full around, Bolan saw that the big blond man had cut across the compound and was standing to one side, the Luger raised in both hands in firing-range stance.

Bolan spun the wheel hard to the left just as the handgun boomed.

White-hot pain seared across Bolan's right shoulder, now hit a second time.

By then the man in black had the Beretta out. He squeezed off two quick shots and saw Paradine fall and roll, but he could not be sure the man was hit. Bolan swerved back on course, and the Jeep shot out through the ragged hole in the fence where the gate had been. Billowing dust obscured his backtrack.

Bolan careened around the first switchback. Adamian clambered into the seat beside him.

"Are you all right?" Bolan asked.

The other man stared at him, his face grim and drawn, and the realization of all the death he had just been a party to—suddenly overtook him. His shoulders slumped, and he stared at the floorboards with unseeing eyes.

"Close enough," Bolan growled.

He took the second hairpin turn, flicked on the Jeep's headlights, and peered into the darkness for one very changed ex-presidential aide and one very special woman.

24

Bolan was aware of the cool fingers as soon as they touched him. To another person he probably appeared unconscious. Actually, he was catching a little of what he called combat sleep. His senses remained alert, while his body was able to nourish itself with the rest it had been denied for so long. Sure, the mission was over, but Bolan had not survived a life of combat by letting down his guard.

The fingers were probing at his shoulder, which ached. He opened his eyes to the dim light inside the stone hut of Kabrina's people, then looked up at the girl herself.

"It's time we had a look at that," she said. "I would have done it sooner, but you were breathing well and there was no fever, so I thought the rest would do you as much good as anything."

Bolan sat up. Kabrina's mother and grandmother were sitting on the same bench at the wall, wearing the same dour expressions, as if they had never moved at all.

"Hold still," Kabrina commanded. She tore a wider gap in the stretch material of the blacksuit, revealing the spot where Bolan had slapped a medicated field compress on the earlier wound. The new gash was within an inch of the first.

"I hope you've got a good tailor," the girl said.

"I've got a good nurse."

She grinned at the compliment, and the fingers probed again. "They're not very deep," she said. "There isn't any muscle or bone missing. If you ever had a chip on your shoulder, it's gone now!"

Bolan laughed and watched the girl bathe and rebandage the wounds, taking in her fine-featured dark face as she worked over him. When she was done, she gave the dressing a gentle pat and Bolan a grin.

"Kabrina," he said seriously. "We'll be leaving in a few minutes."

"You'd better," she said lightly. "My father and uncles will be down from the high country this afternoon, and when they hear the story mother has to tell them, well.... You may be tough enough to face a regiment of Turkish revolutionaries, but I don't think you'd want to face them."

She was grinning, but Bolan knew that what had happened the night before was burned forever into her memory cells. The smiles would still come, but never as easily as before he had come into her life.

"Apologize to them for me," Bolan said. "The women and the men. For whatever good it might do, tell them that you helped stop a very bad thing, one that would have touched even them."

He stood up and bowed to the women. Kabrina spoke to them briefly, then took Bolan's arm.

"Someday I'll leave this place," she said. "Will I see you again?"

Bolan looked down at this lovely woman, wise beyond her years. "If not in this world, Kabrina, I'll look for you in the next."

He put his hands on her shoulders and kissed her lightly on the lips, oblivious to the staring women. "Live large, Kabrina," he said.

Hagen was crouched at the edge of the little yard. He stood up when Bolan came out of the hut, and nodded toward Adamian. The big Armenian was sitting with his back to the wall, his arms circling his drawn-up legs, the look of misery tinged with confusion on his face denying the bright sunrise of what promised to be a fine spring day.

"I don't think he slept at all last night," Hagen said quietly as he came up to Bolan. "He's been sitting there like that since I got up."

Adamian looked up suddenly at Bolan, his eyes wide and watery.

"The Turk," he said.

Bolan crouched beside him.

"The little Turk," Adamian said. "The girl says his name was Horuk."

"Yes."

"A Turk," Adamian said. "And he gave his life for me."

"That's right."

Adamian looked up, his eyes pleading for the relief of understanding. "But he was a Turk," he repeated.

"Hook learned something, Adamian," Bolan said. "You'd better learn the same thing. Sure, your ancestors were slaughtered like cattle by the Turks, and no one is asking you to forget that. But Hook and his ancestors were forced to live lives of subjugation and poverty, and that's worth remembering as well."

Bolan lit two cigarettes and handed one to the other man. Adamian took a deep drag.

"What Hook learned is that *nations* don't oppress people," Bolan went on more gently. "*People* oppress people. Hook was a man—a special kind of man. The kind of man who was not only able to recognize the right side, but was willing to fight for it as well. There aren't too many of those left in the world."

Adamian nodded his head slowly.

"You think about it," Bolan pressed. "You'll realize that you and Hook were a lot more alike than you were different. Maybe you had reason to think he was your enemy, but you were wrong. He was your brother."

Adamian pulled himself to his feet, then reached out to enfold Bolan in his embrace.

"I'll say amen to that," Hagen said from the sidelines, breaking the awkward silence.

Bolan stepped back and looked at Adamian, then at Hagen.

"Let's go home," he said.

SARGE ---

BAD SITUATION IN MINNEAPOLIS. TONI CRITICALLY INJURED RESULT OF PERSONAL ASSAULT BY UNKNOWN. CHECK YOU LATER WITH DETAILS.

POL

CODE BLUE
FROM STONYMAN FARM 081117E
TO NSC/BROGNOLA WASHDC
BT
PHOENIX SENDS X SHOW ME STANDDOWN 24 HOURS
URGENT PERSONAL BUSINESS MINNEAPOLIS AREA X
TONI BLANCANALES GRAVELY INJURED APPARENT
VICTIM OF QUOTE MINNEAPOLIS MANGLER UNQUOTE
X STONYMAN TWO IN CHANGE PENDING RETURN
BT
EOM

CODE BLUE
FROM STONYMAN FARM 081825E
TO NSC/BROGNOLA WASHDC
BT
APRIL SENDS SCRAMBLER RELAY PHOENIX TO
BROGNOLA 081815E X MPLS SITUATION COMMANDS
CLOSE LOOK X STAND ME DOWN STONYMAN MISSIONS
UFN AND CODE ALL REDFLAG TRAFFIC ATTN PHOENIX
FORCE PENDING MPLS RESOLUTION X END RELAY X
STONYMAN TWO COVERING REDFLAG SITUATIONS AT
STONYMAN X ADVISE NO INTERFERENCE MPLS BUT
SUGGEST ALERT LOCAL LEA HIS PRESENCE IN TWIN
CITIES AREA TO PRECLUDE POSSIBLY DANGEROUS
CONFRONTATION X STRIKER MISSION REPEAT
STRIKER MISSION
BT
EOM

CODE BLUE
FROM WHITE HOUSE 081850E
TO STONYMAN TWO
BT
BROGNOLA SENDS FOR SCRAMBLER RELAY PHOENIX
FIRST OPPORTUNITY X AMERICA ONE DISTURBED
POSSIBLE LEGAL RAMIFICATIONS STRIKER
MISSION IN DOMESTIC THEATRE BUT UNDERSTANDS
PERSONAL NATURE INVOLVEMENT X URGES LOW
PROFILE AND ALL POSSIBLE RESTRAINT X LEA
ALERTED WITH TENTATIVE AGREEMENT
NONINTERFERENCE DEPENDENT UPON LOW PROFILE X
EXTEND REGRETS TO BLANCANALES AND ASSURE HIM
FULL RESOURCES THIS OFFICE AT HIS DISPOSAL X
KEEP US INFORMED
BT
EOM

MACK BOLAN

THE EXECUTIONER 41

The Violent Streets

Mack Bolan's Lear jet arrives in St. Paul in the middle of a violent thunderstorm. It is a warning, an electrifying foretaste of the deadly events to come.

Old friend and crime-fighting vet Rosario Blancanales meets Bolan at the airport. His kid sister, Toni, has been horribly raped, but at least she is still alive—unlike five other girls in the city, whose bodies have been found nude, brutally beaten, throats slashed.

It is murder times five, and an attack on someone close. Certainly not a global isssue, but more than enough to fire up the old rage deep in Bolan's gut. Then the policewoman in charge of Toni's rape case is kidnapped. Things begin to look more complex. Someone is obviously out to stop a rape investigation at all costs.

Bolan's intuitive analysis of events indicates this is more than a mad killer on the loose. But what...why? Ruthlessly stalking the kidnappers, Mack Bolan blazes a bloody trail that leads, shockingly, back to the police station itself—and a gruesome cover-up operation!

Someone high up in law-enforcement echelons knows the identity of the murdering rapist—and is prepared to keep the secret. A psychopathic killer now had the license to rape, maim and kill. Even in the grimmest chapters of Bolan's war on crime, this ranks as one of the most sickening cases.

Mack Bolan has to stop it. He must end this rotten game and destroy all the players. There will be no intermission, no pardons, no excuses. Bolan will once again be judge, jury . . . and executioner.